# Northern Exposure

*Compass Brothers, Book 1*

*Jayne Rylon and Mari Carr*

ISBN: 978-1-941785-48-5

Editor: Amy Sherwood

Cover Artist: Jayne Rylon

Print          Formatting:          Mari          Carr

*All roads lead home when that's where you've left your heart.*

Silas Compton always had his eye on Lucy, the veterinarian's daughter. He was even content to wait for the girl of his dreams to grow up before getting anywhere near her with his family's double-edged legacy.

Waiting around led to fooling around with his best friend—and an impulsive eruption of desire that Lucy's innocent eyes weren't meant to see. Figuring Compton Pass wasn't big enough for either the three of them or the pain he'd caused, Silas let loose his tightly reined wanderlust and headed for Alaska.

Ten years later, when an oil rig accident sends him home, he braces himself for the reopening of old wounds. Instead he finds himself in the care—and welcoming arms—of Lucy and Colby, whose marriage has plenty of room for the man they both still love. And forgive with all their hearts.

As things start to unravel at Compass Ranch, Silas must dig deep for the strength to assume his rightful place in the Compton family...and lay the foundation for a future with his lovers. If he can forgive himself.

Warning: This book is overflowing with sexy cowboys who like to saddle up and ride each other as well as the woman of their dreams. The likelihood of becoming addicted to their ranch family is high. With three more stories yet to come, beware. You won't be able     to     read     just     one!

# Prologue

Dry brush crackled under the hooves of Silas Compton's roan gelding. It hadn't rained in a while. He could tell it would be a long summer by the clouds of terra cotta dust rising in the wake of his brothers's galloping horses as they raced across the mountain ridge.

Not that he'd know it where he was headed. Alaska would provide a total change of scenery. Exactly what he needed. Pain lanced his chest, causing him to tense in his heirloom saddle. Rainey's ears flicked up. Silas patted the loyal animal's neck, settling into the rhythm of their canter, and wondered how he would survive so far from the land that had been a part of him since he'd been born.

Somehow he would have to make it work.

He sure as hell couldn't stay.

Like the three-legged dog they'd had as kids, he would learn to cope without an integral part of himself. If only he and his puppy had reined in their curiosity and avoided those damn traps…

But they hadn't.

Lucy Silver, the veterinarian's sweet daughter—who'd been dancing through his dirty dreams since he'd been old enough to have them—had spotted Silas making out with her boyfriend in the barn. It'd been like the day he'd watched his puppy scramble toward the razor-sharp jaws lying concealed under a pile of straw all over again.

Removing himself from the equation seemed like the only way he could halt imminent disaster and protect the two people he cared about most outside of his family. He'd already destroyed enough of Lucy's innocence.

Christ, he couldn't explain what had driven him to kiss Colby in the first place.

Impulsive. Rash. Reckless.

Qualities Silas didn't value. The one time he gave in to the dark urges he wrestled, he paid a horrible price. But he'd caught Colby checking out his sweaty muscles as they'd worked together in the heat of the day. Desire had arced between them.

Irresistible. Delicious. Forbidden.

Until the agony on Lucy's face had slammed him back to reality. Silas vowed to leave the couple to mend their fences and live in peace, without the threat of his interference ripping them apart. Lucy and Colby devoured each other with desperate gazes when they thought no one paid attention. It didn't take a genius to figure out their love was the real deal.

He'd go, even if it meant giving up everything familiar and cherished, including his brothers and his two best friends. Because he sure as shit couldn't stay and keep his hands to himself. Not with a double helping of temptation running wild.

Amber rays from the setting sun ignited the prairie below. The glowing grasslands seared into his memory. He'd never lose track of his roots. He'd never forget his heritage, Compass Ranch, even if he couldn't accept his destiny as its head.

His brothers would pick up his slack.

Seth, a year younger than him, whooped then grinned over his shoulder as he spurred his mare faster. Wild as a mustang, he flew over the landscape to the spot they'd claimed as their own. The twins, Sam and Sawyer, followed suit.

They hadn't discussed their plans for the evening. As soon as Silas had made his announcement to the family, the boys had glanced around the dining table— where all important family business was conducted— and nodded. They hadn't objected to his desertion, but strain lined their faces, sorrow dimmed their eyes and the betrayal he feared flashed in the air a split second before they began planning how they'd support him.

Christ, their generosity had made him feel lower than the shit on the bottom of his muck boots because he hadn't had the guts to admit why he really planned to leave. None of *them* would have been dumb enough to mess with something that wasn't theirs. And if they had, they wouldn't have lied about it on top. Such strong souls would thrive with or without him. But could he cut out something so essential to his being and live so wounded? So lost?

Cut adrift, he might not make it.

Silas gripped the reins too tight. He forced himself to relax his fingers.

One night. He'd give himself these final hours with his brothers to say goodbye to all he treasured. Tomorrow, he'd ride out. Forever.

The driving hoof beats slowed as they approached their destination. By the time they ducked beneath the shelter of the mountain cypresses, the rocky terrain forced them to walk their mounts. None of the teenagers would jeopardize the safety of their animals or their brothers.

He squeezed his eyes shut, trying to contain the agony lassoing his heart as he realized he'd never be close to the men they'd grow into, their families or the children who'd take their places in the tight-knit community like so many generations before them.

The last damn thing he wanted was to bawl like a sissy.

If his family caught on to his pain, they might not let him go. Luckily, he'd learned from the toughest sons of bitches in the west how to be a real cowboy. If that was the only way he could honor his legacy, he'd man up and do it. Somehow.

They dismounted, reverting to familiar patterns. Seth and Sawyer tied the horses as Sam gathered kindling for their bonfire. Silas patched the pit left from prior visits then dug some supplies from his pack, including hot dogs despite the fact they'd eaten dinner before they left. These days, the four of them could shovel in enough to feed an army.

Or so their mom said.

"Si, you're bleeding." Count on Sawyer to notice.

"It's nothing." Silas faced the youngest, by twenty-two minutes, of his brothers. The kid's twin had already picked up on the vibe. Damn their weird-ass mental connection.

"It's something." Sam sidled up behind him to take a peek. "It's too uniform to be a cut."

"Did you do it?" Damn if Seth didn't tip his hat and glare from beneath his dark brows. When Silas didn't answer, Seth stomped over. "Holy shit. You did. You got a freaking tattoo. Without me? Without us? You asshole!"

Silas dodged his brother's half-hearted punch toward the sore spot between his shoulder blades. The disappointment radiating from the guy in waves did more damage than his fist would have. After Silas's sudden declaration of independence, this looked bad, but he couldn't come clean and admit the craving he'd had to brand himself with some symbol of home before he took off. Not if he had any hope of escaping.

"I had a hard enough time convincing Snake to ink me. If I'd brought you guys with me, he never would have caved. He only did it because I'm eighteen now."

If Silas had told Seth, they wouldn't have been able to stop Sam and Sawyer from tagging along too.

"Well, I suppose that's true. Plus he's probably afraid JD will kill him if he finds out." Sawyer let Silas off easy, as usual.

"Yeah, that's why I took the bandages off. Didn't want him to notice."

Pride for their badass father glowed from the kid. Silas agreed. As head of Compass Ranch—the center of Compton Pass, Wyoming—JD Compton wielded vast financial clout but his personality made him larger than life and, most important, earned him respect by the acre.

"But you gotta let us see it at least," Sawyer insisted.

"Sure." Silas dropped a wedge of firewood on the crackling flame Sam had started, and then stood. All three of his brothers lined up behind him—Seth in the middle, the twins on either side—when he tugged his gray T-shirt over his head, wincing a little at the sting of his sweat in the open wound. The three usually raucous kids didn't make a single peep when he revealed the artwork. "It's swollen and stuff—"

"Whoa." Seth broke the silence.

"It's awesome." Sam laid his palm to the right of the emblem, careful not to touch the raw skin.

"Sweet," Sawyer agreed then added his hand on the left side of Silas's back.

"Does it hurt?" Seth completed their connection, touching the area below the design.

"So bad," Silas gasped, struggling not to drop to his knees.

"I'm still doing it. Next year. The minute I turn eighteen," Seth whispered into the gathering twilight. "Exactly like this."

"Me too," Sam chimed in. "The compass design is fucking great. And the ranch brand is perfect. It matches the one we use."

"I didn't know Snake had this kind of shit in him. The shading is so cool. It looks 3-D." Sawyer's hand shook on Silas's back. "I want one now. Like yours. But without the fancy N."

"You're only fifteen," Silas barked. "Wait a while and make sure it's what you really want."

"I know what I want."

"Things don't always happen like you expect, Sawyer." Silas felt the pressure of his brothers' hands bracing him as he heaved a giant sigh.

"Is that why you're leaving?" The high pitch of Sam's question reminded Silas that even though his youngest brothers had started fooling around with girls in their class, and he'd busted them splitting a six pack they'd swiped from the bunkhouse, they still had more boy than man in them.

"Yeah." He couldn't give them more of the truth than that. It embarrassed him. Angered him. And threatened to drown him in despair.

"Well, some people might flip flop around. Not me. Not going to change *my* mind." Sawyer stuck to his guns. He'd always been the most determined to prove himself despite being the baby of the group. Maybe because of it. "I'm joining the Coast Guard. Gonna see the world."

"What?" Silas pivoted to stare at the kid, severing the connection with his brothers. He regretted it instantly, but he had to search Sawyer's eyes for the truth. "You've been watching too many freaking commercials. Your place is here, on the ranch."

"No, it isn't," the teenager whispered.

When the other two nodded in agreement, Silas staggered backward.

"You're not planning to stay?" His forehead crumpled as he tried to understand. "None of you?"

"Don't look at us like that." Seth waved his hands in front of his chest. "I figured you'd understand. I need to get the hell out of here. Find my own place. Same as you. Not Alaska though, I hate winter. You're crazy to take on all that snow. Somewhere warm. Maybe I'll head down south. Yeah, that's what I'll do. A fancy S instead of an N on my compass, bro."

"What? No!" Silas couldn't explain. "It's not like that. I mean—"

"We understand, Si." Sam smiled then nodded. "I'd like to go to college. Earn a degree, find a real job. Something where I don't have to dirty my hands to rake in cash. I'll have fancy clothes, a slick apartment and a kickass car. I'll party every night with the hottest girls in the city."

The relief washing over his brothers filled Silas with anxiety and left him reeling. Who would help their father with the ranch? Who would continue their family traditions? Who if not him? Or Seth? Or Sam?

"Oh, no." Sawyer shook his head as he kicked a rock. "Don't give me that look. I told you, I'm *not* getting stuck here. Fuck that. You think someone should hang around, then stay put. It ain't too late to cancel your plane ticket."

"I-I can't."

"And neither can we." Seth slugged his shoulder. "Come on, start the dogs. I'm starving. Jake slipped me a couple Playboys for doing his chores last weekend so he could bang Misty Trelane."

"Nice! Me first." Sam managed a head start for their brother's backpack as Sawyer launched himself after his twin.

Silas watched them wrestle, laugh and call each other names as though his entire world hadn't been ripped apart. Then he pivoted and stared out to the horizon as the sun set on his childhood.

# Chapter One

*Ten Years Later*

Silas frowned into a cracked, empty glass as the burn of whiskey permeated his chest, faking a warmth he hadn't experienced in a decade. He slammed the tumbler on the shitty plank bar then motioned for another. A few more and he might actually believe he languished in the middle of a perfect Wyoming summer.

But what would be the point?

He'd wake tomorrow morning, miserable and lonely as usual.

He studied the fresh picture hanging, a little crooked, on the Wall of Death. Macabre? Maybe. But the lifers who came to Alaska to seek out her dangerous jobs formed a kind of brotherhood where each member understood that, for some, a tragic early ending came as a welcome relief. They all ran from something—war wounds, screwed up childhoods, a life of monotony—God only knew what.

In addition to the misfits, a few others rounded out the mix. Foolish men and women, who didn't comprehend the risks, attempted to make a quick buck. Adrenaline junkies on a permanent high soared from hazard to hazard. Still, for the most part, broken men littered the gorgeous, frozen landscape.

Silas saluted the deceased captain of the crabbing boat with his refilled glass then downed the next dose of poison too. Despite his tarnished past, Captain Robert had saved Silas's ass a time or two during the tours Silas had served harvesting on the vessel before he moved on to long haul driving along treacherous routes. He remembered the screams he'd heard on occasion when the captain had a particularly bad night and the times they'd drunk themselves into oblivion to avoid the darkness a little longer.

Hopefully the man had found peace at last.

He started a mental list of all the comrades he'd lost in the extreme positions he'd mastered—expedition guide, crabber, big rig driver and pilot on top of his current gig as an oil rig motorhand. After several dozen, their faces blurred in his mind.

Could have something to do with all the alcohol he'd consumed in those ten years. Or the numbness infecting his soul as he wandered so far from the place and people he loved.

Silas glowered in an attempt to scare off the woman headed straight for his permanent spot at the dive. In this mood, he'd make no kind of company for a lady.

"Knock it off, Compass." Red, nicknamed for the bright jacket he wore on the job, elbowed Silas's ribs. "I'll take her off your hands if you're not hungry. It's been a long time since I had a meal that fine."

Silas squinted, trying to focus despite the solid drunk he'd been heading toward. Red had a point. A sweet thing like her didn't wander into their territory often. In fact, women in general were in short supply here, at the end of the world.

The deficit made him long for the squandered plenty of his youth. And provided the perfect opportunity for him to slake his lust for men.

Rough, raw craving would build inside him for months until he surrendered to gnawing need. Companionship came at a high price around here for most men, but once rumors of Silas's edge had spread, he'd had a line of willing partners a pointed look and a nod away.

For the past six months or so, he'd spent the majority of his off time with Red. The man made it easy on him, never asking for more than Silas could give. After the first time they'd hooked up—when Silas had allowed the man to suck him off in the bar's grimy bathroom—Red had made it clear he'd welcome a quick fuck in the back of a truck, a shared night with some woman they happened across or whatever else suited Silas's violent mood swings.

Silas never allowed himself to take advantage of the more generous offers lurking in Red's eyes, though. Shit. Those emotions grew day by day. He dropped his head in his hands, spearing his fingers through his unkempt hair as he realized he'd have to distance himself from his roommate before the man got hurt. He'd move out after their double shift this weekend.

Two people and two people alone inspired more than carnal savagery in him. It wouldn't be fair to give Red hope that Silas's longing for Lucy and Colby would change in this lifetime. If ten years hadn't killed his dedication, nothing would.

Hell, Silas couldn't bear companionship some days. He didn't remember how to be a friend. It'd been too many years. Pride in a hard day's work and the reassuring discomfort of a solid hangover, which insured he'd passed out for at least a few hours before heading to the job to do it all over again, propelled him forward through week after week.

"Your friend looks like he could use some

cheering up."

Why in the hell did his surly temper attract women like bees to honey? It seemed the more he growled and tried to warn them off, the more they wanted in his pants. Insane. Every one of them. Just like him.

"And what about me?" Red turned to the woman with his best imitation of Silas's genuine misery. "Maybe *I* need some of your healing touch."

"Don't worry, handsome. I'm the kind of woman who can handle two strapping men at once."

The sassy introduction made the corner of Silas's mouth curve up despite his resolve. Tough Alaskan women reminded him of Wyoming cowgirls in a hell of a lot of ways.

Sexy ways.

Here, like home, the imbalance in the population of men and women made folks open to some interesting possibilities. He glanced at the brazen woman out the corner of his eye. Through vision blurred by windburn and too many fingers of Jack, she bore a slight resemblance to Lucy.

At least, how Silas imagined the woman of his dreams might look today. A riot of red-gold curls and bright blue eyes had his cock hard in an instant.

How had he gone so long without seeing her? His parents? His brothers?

His stagnant life disgusted him. Working toward someone else's dream. No land to show for it. Nothing like his great-great-grandfather had built and no one to pass it on to anyway. Just fistfuls of cash and far too many meaningless fucks. That might not have seemed so bad in his early twenties, but he'd be thirty soon for Christ's sake.

"Lucky for you, Silas and I like to play hard too."

"Not tonight, Red." Silas shook his head then

shoved from the bar. He staggered two steps toward the door before his bunkmate and the cute barfly chased after him. "Count me out."

His friend's jaw went slack.

"Shush, Si." The woman's soft entreaty teased the side of his neck.

Shit, no one had called him that in ages. He didn't give a shit how she'd found out his name. He had a reputation around these parts.

It sounded...nice. Right.

"Let me make you feel good then tuck you in." The woman ducked beneath his arm and plastered herself against his side. Her soft breasts covered in a fuzzy sweater cushioned his ribs. Without thought, his hand dropped to her ass.

Maybe she had a decent idea. Some of his desperation morphed into desire, relieving the pressure on his heart. Still, as the front door banged open and they piled into Red's all-wheel drive truck, he cautioned the minx.

"I'm in one hell of a mood tonight, sugar." He couldn't be sure she'd heard since she didn't pause her exploration of his jaw on her path to his lips. He stopped her before she attempted to engage in mouth to mouth. Ever since Colby he hadn't indulged in the intimacy.

She straddled him, grinding against his erection through his jeans.

He took her delicate shoulders in his hands and shook a bit until her gaze met his. "Do you understand?"

She paused and a slow smile spread across her plump lips when she noticed the beast straining to slip its chains. He couldn't hide the feral desire in his eyes. Not that close.

"I won't be gentle," Silas growled.

"Promise?" She bit her lip. "Is it so difficult to believe I *like* it rough, Compass? I heard you could give me what I need."

Gravel pinged off the exterior of the truck as Red departed in a lurch for the seedy dorms a bunch of the oil workers shared. Not having a place of his own to take a woman had never bothered Silas before. Tonight it did.

He wanted to make her scream.

He was too old for this clandestine nonsense.

"Amuse yourselves for a bit. I'll have us there in twenty minutes." Red careened along the treacherous roadway, dodging snowdrifts and frozen road kill. He peeked over at them groping each other every couple seconds.

Silas decided to give the man a show. He flipped the truck's heater to the max then unzipped the woman's down vest. He shoved the puffy, ice blue garment from her shoulders before burrowing his hands beneath her sweater. Her satiny skin seared his work-roughened fingers. She didn't squeak or flinch when the calloused surface of his palms scraped her nipples.

Instead, she moaned then arched closer. Her hips rocked, searching for some contact on her pussy. Even through the layers she wore, he could smell her arousal.

"Mmm, you're a dirty girl, aren't you?" He pinched the puckered tips of her breasts.

Hard.

"The sweetest looking ones always are." She tilted her head then purred, "Haven't you figured that out by now?"

If only her theory were true then Lucy wouldn't have fled when she'd caught him and Colby messing around. One moment had changed the course of his life forever. If Lucy had stayed, or come closer—curious— he and Colby could have taken turns gifting her with pleasure after pleasure.

Silas had already brought the hungry woman on his lap to multiple orgasms, wishing she truly was the girl he longed for, by the time they reached their quarters. He refused to call the shithole home. Only one place deserved that honor, and it sure as hell wasn't some cinderblock dormitory in the middle of frozen-fucking-nowhere.

He threw her over his shoulder and strode for the back of the building. Red ran ahead to their window, hopping through the pane they left unlocked most nights they went out. No matter how rough their fuckmate liked things, flaunting an eager woman to an entire crew of isolated, horny men suffering eternal boredom couldn't be forgiven.

Silas wrapped his hands around her dainty waist then handed her to Red. After he pulled himself up and through, he shut the window tight, covering it with thermal protectors. Hands on hips, he took stock of the situation. The ride had sobered him some, enough to assess his two willing partners, who ripped each other's clothes off on the bare mattress in front of him.

He crossed the ten meager steps to their door, which opened into the dorm's hallway. After a quick check through the peephole, he wedged a chair beneath the knob. Things could get loud. He wouldn't chance anyone coming to investigate, hoping to bust in on the action. In the past decade, he'd had to fight off more than a few overzealous brutes.

Despite his less than sterling track record, he wouldn't stand for a woman to be hurt. Unless he inflicted controlled pain that detonated an explosion of rapture.

From the steady slaps and moans behind him, he figured Red had a head start in that department. Silas let the man have his fun because once he joined the game, the tables would turn and Red would beg to please him. It happened without fail.

Memories of the man bending over for Silas had precome dribbling from the head of his cock. He padded toward the couple wrestling on the sagging bed. In the glow from the bare bulb over the can—the sole light in the room—his mind played cruel tricks. Red and their hookup resembled Colby and Lucy.

Why had he never noticed that about Red before? Maybe his subconscious obscured the real reason he'd allowed the man to worm closer than anyone in years. Silas stroked his stiffening shaft and permitted his imagination to run wild.

"Get on your hands and knees, baby." Red directed the woman to present herself to Silas. "He loves to fuck from behind."

His roommate spread the woman's legs until her pussy lips separated, the moist tissue glistening in the diffuse light. Silas didn't lose concentration as he reached to the table beside the bed for a condom, ripped it open with his teeth then rolled the latex over his throbbing cock.

"She's had enough teasing, Compass." The other man dipped his fingers in the drenched slit awaiting him. When its owner cried out, Red painted her arousal over her clit, playing with the sensitive nerves there. "Take her."

How could he resist a gift like that? Silas pretended the wanton beckoning him was Lucy. *His* Lucy. The girl he'd grown up with, shared his aspirations with, known from the first instant could handle the rough Wyoming lifestyle. The woman he'd lost before he'd had a chance to make her his own.

He shucked his shirt then nudged the waistband of his unbuttoned his jeans.

"Jesus, that never gets old. Wait 'til you see him,

honey. He's gorgeous."

Silas's pants dropped to the floor.

"A bonus, for sure. But I'm more concerned with how he fucks. I need it. Bad."

Silas practically ran to the bed then leaped upon it. If he had it to do over again, he'd make sure she never went without. He'd stake a claim so primal she'd never dare to date another man. No, he'd establish a bond so essential she'd thrive in the aftermath of his attention and that of the man he'd come to realize he craved equally.

Silas wrapped the fingers of one hand in the hair of the woman. With the other, he shackled Red's wrist and guided the fervent man to surround his cock. His partner understood what he demanded.

Red caressed the thick hard-on in his grasp, aligning the purple tip with the entrance of the woman's pussy. The first touch of Silas's cock on the woman's hot flesh threatened to scald him through the thin barrier protecting them both. They all moaned their approval. Red fed Silas's erection to the woman, using her ample arousal to lubricate the thick, veined shaft.

When all of Silas's length tucked into the humid channel, he shifted his hips so his balls rested on Red's hand. The man cupped him. Red peered up at Silas, his head tilted, awaiting orders.

"Get down there," Silas barked. "Lay on your back between our legs. Suck my balls. Lick her. Make it good. I'm going to ride her hard. She better come before I do or your ass will be too sore to sit tomorrow."

He saw the momentary debate waging in Red. The man must have considered disobeying him on purpose. He relished a tinge of pain with his pleasure. In the end, he complied as though he could tell Silas wasn't in the mood for games tonight.

No, Silas needed the real thing. If he didn't find an outlet for the rage and frustration building inside, he'd shatter. Thank God his bedmates required the same.

The woman writhed on Silas's impaling cock, trying to shove him deeper as she ground herself on Red's face. When his roommate's tongue lapped along the center seam of his sac, Silas pulled out of the woman's pussy, drawing his cock across the eager muscle licking juice from his full-blown erection.

He changed direction, sinking inside the woman once more, loving the pressure that built on his plump head before it squeezed past the clenched ring of muscle guarding her entrance. She shrieked as he bottomed out with one fierce push.

Silas set a rhythm none of them could withstand for long. He blanketed the woman's back, biting her shoulder when he realized she smelled like Lucy too. Strawberry shampoo always propelled him to the brink of madness. He pounded her pussy, gauging her excitement from her pants, which edged toward screams. The talented manipulation of Red's tongue over her clit and Silas's balls enhanced his assault.

Silas ran one hand along her waist, up her center then filled his palm with her breast. He squeezed hard, concentrating on driving through her tightening grasp.

"You like that. Don't you, Lu?" He growled in her ear and redoubled his strokes.

"Damn straight. Except my name isn't—"

Colby must have nipped her to cut her off so quick. He whispered, "Don't ruin Compass's fantasy."

Lucy nodded then shuddered beneath Silas as Colby resumed his treatment. When Silas sensed her hovering on the verge of orgasm, he knelt upright, never altering his course inside her clinging sheath.

"Harder?" he roared then jammed his hand

beneath her.

Colby sucked the finger Silas extended, coating it with saliva and the excess from their partner's soaked pussy.

"Yes!" Lucy surrendered. Her whole body went lax in his hold, allowing his cock to plunder a fraction of an inch deeper. "Make me come. Oh, God. Please. Make me come."

Silas yanked his finger from Colby, allowing the man to return to his exploration of Lucy's clit. He spread her cheeks wide with one hand then notched the tip of his spit-soaked finger in her ass. She rocked toward him at the same time he inserted his digit in her tight, hot hole.

Then she spasmed, choking his cock and his finger, threatening to drown Colby between their legs. She wailed. Her tremors continued for long minutes as he fucked her with slower, steady passes, massaging her clenching passage. When at last she sighed, he pulled free. A viscous strand of her fluids stretched between them, decorating Colby's cheek.

The man swiped the evidence of their debauchery from his face then ingested her pleasure. He never blinked, never took his stare from Silas's raging hard-on. "My turn? Please, Compass?"

"Damn straight, Colby."

The man prepared Silas, stripping the condom from his cock and replacing it with a fresh one in a matter of seconds. When he flipped onto his knees at the speed of light, Silas chuckled. "So eager. Is that cock of yours nice and hard? Let me see."

Colby whimpered and rolled to his side next to their recovering mate. Sure enough, his cock stuck straight out—red and defined by his lust.

"Very nice." Silas smiled as he inspected the man's tool. "It'd be a shame to waste a quality boner like that. Lu, you want more?"

Lucy cracked her heavy eyelids and grinned. She rotated to her back then spread her arms and legs in welcome.

"You want me to fuck her?" Colby verified, unwilling to risk misbehaving.

"Get in there. Put that cock in her pussy so I can fuck you both at the same time." A rush of pure adrenaline more potent than ten bottles of whiskey made him drunk on pleasure as he watched Colby suit up then slide home.

The motion of his partner's hips as he screwed deeper on every pass was jerky—not as refined as Silas's expert fucking—but that didn't keep Lucy from whimpering as Colby's hard-on stimulated the swollen walls of her ultra-sensitive pussy.

"There you go." Silas petted Colby's flank as he pressed tight to their woman, his cock embedded as far as he could reach. "That's the way."

Without warning, Silas dropped a resounding spank on Colby's ass. The slap of his palm reverberated throughout the room. Colby lunged forward, forcing a cry from Lucy beneath him. Silas grinned then did it again, and again, until the man's ass glowed red in the artificial twilight of the room and Lucy's restless heels drumming on the bed proclaimed her ready for another round.

Silas leaned over and snagged a half-empty bottle of lube from the table beside the bed. The cool gel soothed his flaming palm as he slathered it over the length of his cock.

"Hurry." Colby grunted as Silas fucked in tiny strokes, trying to hang on. "I'm not going to last much longer."

He didn't have to ask twice.

Silas pressed his hard-on into Colby's crack then

clenched Colby's ass as he tipped his hips forward. He kept the bulbous head of his cock from popping out of the tight ring of muscle with two fingers on the top of his shaft while he overcame the man's last resistance. Once the ridge of his fat head penetrated the tissue strangling it, he sank several inches deep in one thrust.

Colby shouted then drove forward into Lucy. Silas watched her nails dig into the exposed skin over his partner's shoulders, leaving half-moon indentations as proof of her approval. That she enjoyed her men fucking did more to arouse him than any of the delicious friction they generated together.

Silas pumped his cock into the depths of Colby's ass, massaging the man's gland repeatedly. The powerful body beneath him began to tremble. Lucy soothed Colby, urging him to come in her pussy, accepting the dark desires that ensnared them all.

She shouted her satisfaction at the same time Colby milked Silas's cock with his ass as his orgasm struck. Assured he'd pleased his partners, Silas allowed his restraint to evaporate. He flooded the condom nestled in the man's back passage with spurt after spurt of his seed and still his climax continued.

He closed his eyes and floated, nearly weeping with the joy he found in sharing himself with his lovers.

For a few seconds he embraced the heat, thawing his heart. Until he crashed to earth and realized the pair in his bed weren't his lovers at all but merely his roommate and some willing woman they'd carted home from a bar.

"Son of a bitch." He ripped himself from Red's still shuddering body and dropped to his knees on the floor beside the bed. A wave of nausea assaulted him, but he swallowed the bile burning his throat.

In the background he heard Red whispering to the drowsy woman in his arms. It added another weight to

Silas's conscience to inconvenience her when she'd been so generous, but he couldn't stand to return and pretend the couple in his bed was comprised of the people he craved.

Even after all this time.

Some things *never* changed.

"Get dressed, honey. I'll take you home." Red gathered the thong dangling from their gear stacked in the corner before helping her arrange the rest of her clothes. "If you want to snuggle up there, I'm game."

"But Compass..."

"He always sleeps alone."

# Chapter Two

Red lights swirled across the steel structure, casting eerie shadows as the whine of sirens scared sane men toward the exit. Silas grabbed a helmet, a fire jacket and a hatchet from the supply station then fought against the current, deeper into the rig. The incessant scream of the emergency warning and the *clomp* of work boots on the riveted grate walkway made it impossible to hear anything above the racket but he caught a glimpse of Red in his peripheral vision.

No mistaking that jacket.

He grimaced as he considered the conversation he'd have to have with the man tonight. Investigating a dozen rig fires sounded more appealing than undertaking that task. Christ!

As a motorhand, he could have left this duty to the roustabouts but he always volunteered. Other than a couple minor sparks, which he'd extinguished easily, there'd never been an issue.

Red, on the other hand, could be a problem. Silas didn't do emotions. Not anymore.

Together, the pair wove between the thinning crowds, picking up speed as they burrowed into the belly of the station. Machinery lined the walls of the control room they burst into. Silas shook his head to clear the ringing in his ears when Red slammed the thick door shut behind them, cutting off the roar of the evacuation and dimming the squeal of the alert.

They worked through their checklist, finding no signs of trouble in any of the monitored rooms on camera. Another faulty sensor probably caused the ruckus. They'd had a handful go sour lately. Now they'd have to work two hours longer on a standard eighteen-hour shift to recover the lost time. Not that Silas had anything better to do but some of the guys tired faster than he did and a bunch more couldn't withstand the frigid cold that long.

Mistakes occurred in bad conditions.

"Hey, Compass..."

"You got something?"

"Nah. My side's good to go." Red cleared his throat then continued. "You don't have to explain."

"What?" Silas took his eyes from the instrumentation to glance over his shoulder.

"I can tell you're ready to move on. What I'm sayin' is I know you're done. With me. With us."

"There never was an *us*, Red." Son of a bitch, this was not the time. A bitter taste filled his mouth when his bunkmate flinched. The guy didn't deserve his asshole treatment. "I mean—"

"Don't."

When Silas's eyebrows drew together, the other man explained.

"Don't lie now. You've always been clear you were about no strings and all that shit. It's good. Anyway, I booked a ticket out of here. Ah, you kinda reminded me of what things used to be like. What it could still be like if I quit hiding in deep freeze. I'm going home, Compass. Leaving tonight."

Silas found he couldn't speak around the shock clogging his throat. When he didn't respond, Red swiveled, focusing his attention on the task at hand. Silas did the same as his mind whirled. Red was heading home.

Respect, admiration and envy warred for top billing.

The drill shaft and seven chambers remained to clear. When only two were left, Silas asked, "You think you can go back? To normal stuff? Your old life?"

"I'm gonna try."

"Son of a bitch!" Silas's eyes bulged.

"It ain't *that* crazy—"

"Fire! Sector A. Engine room." He smashed the button used to engage the chemical suppressant system. Nothing happened. "Oh, fuck. It's busted. I'm going in."

"Silas! No!"

If the man tried to persuade him further, the entreaty disappeared beneath the blast of the alarm, which crescendoed when Silas ripped open the door and skidded around the corner toward the site of the trouble.

He leapt over the handrail to the level below rather than take time scrambling down the treacherous incline on the access ladder. Adrenaline made his hefty axe light as a feather in his grasp. He kept running, ignoring the fact that every step put him closer to danger. If he didn't stop the fire from spreading, it would ignite the gas vent in the chamber three doors down.

The men who'd evacuated wouldn't be guaranteed safety. Red and the other crewmembers troubleshooting the alarm from inside would stand no chance. Not to mention the ecological disaster that would follow on the heels of such a catastrophe.

He dropped his shoulders and sprinted, thanking God for each second that passed without an epic kaboom. At least he wouldn't have time to suffer if things ended in the crapper. They'd be obliterated before they had a chance to register their demise.

A Zen-like surrealism cocooned him as he charged along the corridor, thankful he'd kept his affairs in order. If something happened to him, everything important—his parents, his brothers, the ranch, Lucy and Colby—would benefit from the odds he'd beaten for ten years.

He slowed as he neared the pod containing the fire, trailing his fingers along the metal walls to test for conducted heat. Nothing yet. Maybe one of the other guys had coerced the suppression system to kick on.

Or not.

A bang sounded from his left like a rifle shot, spurring him to jump a solid six inches off the ground. Not the mother of all detonations. More like a water pipe bursting as steam built inside it.

Silas tapped his fingers on the door to the engine room. Warm, but not impossible to touch. He had to try to stop the chain of events while he could. He kicked the long steel door handle with the heel of his boot, popping the entrance open even as he ducked to the side.

No flames shot out of the exposed portal. A nervous laugh tumbled from his chest as he figured he'd watched too many movies during the long, dark Alaskan winters.

"You're a crazy bastard, Compass." Red caught up, his breath sawing in ragged gasps that reminded Silas of the time he'd made the man come hard enough he claimed to have seen stars. "Gonna get us both killed and cracking up about it."

"Head out, Red. Tell the rest of the guys what's up. Move them as far away as you can. A bunch of them have families."

"*You* have a family, Compass. You go."

"Don't argue—"

"Not this time. I'm not your bitch anymore." Before Silas could do more than gawk, his bunkmate slapped Silas's ass then darted through the gaping doorway where he disappeared in the thickening haze of smoke.

Silas tugged his shirt over his nose and mouth then dove after Red, his bright jacket blurred by the shimmer of heat waves in the charged air. The clang of metal on metal reverberated through the hiss and pop of flames, which seemed to grow with every slam of Silas's heart against his ribs.

Sparks flew from the junction of Red's axe blade and the pipe running from the fire suppression system, but several mighty blows didn't make enough progress in denting the surface for Silas's liking. He checked over his shoulder. Flames billowed higher and higher— obscuring his vision—in a semi-circle that would soon cut off their exit route.

A fit of coughs threatened to keel him over.

*Fuck this.* They didn't have time. He shoved Red toward the door, knocking the man farther from the worst of the danger. With a roar, Silas laid all his energy into swinging his axe at the black valve capping the end of the pipe.

A plume of chemicals formed a beautiful rooster tail as they sprayed over the blaze, muting the worst of the flames. The angle of saturation didn't quite match the intended zone due to his improvised delivery method. Within seconds, a couple of spots smoldered but the troubling line of fire headed for the main vent had extinguished.

He turned to Red in time to catch the man's grin and fist pump. Backup would be here in no time. They'd clean up the rest. Silas's knees went weak.

How had they ended up so lucky? Insanity would

rule the bar tonight for sure.

Still, the toxic chemicals wreaked havoc on his lungs so he'd wait for later to celebrate. He neared Red, about to pound the man's outstretched fist when his partner's eyes widened.

Silas flew across the room and slammed into something unforgiving before the blast deafened him. His ears rang as he tried to figure out where he was and what had happened. When he struggled to climb to his feet, his left leg gave out, sending a wave of pain crashing over him. He wished he hadn't looked at his thigh when he caught sight of something white poking through his ripped jeans. Blood slicked his hands as he dragged himself along the floor grate, shouting for Red.

The door should be to his right. That's where he thought he'd last seen the man. He snaked across the mangled surface, debris ripping his hide to shreds, but the drive to aid his friend eradicated every other thought.

"Red!" he screamed, but he couldn't hear himself, never mind an answer.

A moment later, a scrap of tattered crimson cloth waved ten feet or so away, beyond the enlarged exit. Somehow, Silas crossed the space in a flash.

Red sat in the hallway, his legs at a funny angle in front of him. A serene smile crossed his face when he spotted Silas dragging himself near.

Thank God.

Then Silas noticed specks of blood dotting the man's face. More and more splatters gathered like obscene freckles. A segment of the railing emerged from Red's chest, where it had impaled him. His jacket, neck and face grew brighter by the second.

"No!" Silas crumpled with his head on his friend's thigh. He couldn't say if blood or tears made the heated tracks down his cheeks.

Red's fingers closed on Silas's elbow, encouraging Silas to use the last of his dazed momentum to roll onto his back and meet the dying man's gaze.

"Go home, Compass."

Silas still couldn't hear. He read the man's trembling, soot-covered lips.

Light faded from Red's eyes. The man refused to quit, fighting to the end. "Before it's too...late."

Silas gasped like a fish out of water, trying to breathe as his friend went limp in his arms. Bright blood seeped from the corner of lips he'd never allowed himself to kiss.

The man's favorite color.

Iron tang overpowered smoke when Silas levered himself up the railing to press his mouth to the man he held. Who had he been trying to kid?

Red hadn't been some meaningless fuck. He'd been a friend.

A damn good one at that. Yet, he'd never have the chance to tell the guy so.

What more had he pretended to be oblivious to?

Silas's life flashed before his eyes, stripping off the illusions he'd crafted. Denial had caused him to forsake all he valued. How much had his family suffered when he severed ties with them despite the infinite love and opportunity they'd lavished on their prodigal firstborn? What had seemed noble for ten years looked selfish as anguish—both physical and mental—seared away his flimsy excuses.

Unforgivable.

The idea of returning home, begging absolution, took root as sparks showered around him and acrid smoke scorched his lungs. Too bad he couldn't move, would never make it out.

Silas collapsed, recalling the faces of each of his

brothers then Lucy and Colby to keep him company in his final moments. A secondary explosion shook the room. He still couldn't make his body react to his demands.

Move! Run! Crawl!

Anything.

Oh God, anything.

Instead, he lay helpless except for the jarring shockwaves from a chain of miniature bangs. The reserve gas tanks, under pressure in the engine room, must have been giving way—one by one.

Flaming bits and metal shrapnel pelted his back as he curled into a ball, refusing to relinquish his connection to Red. When the main tank went, it'd all be over.

At least the fire seemed contained. It hadn't penetrated the chemical barrier they'd laid down or he'd already be toast. Red's sacrifice would not be in vain.

Through moisture not entirely caused by the acrid clouds smothering him, he spotted an open doorway on the level below their landing. His survival instinct stretched, yearning to fly toward the ultra-slim chance, but his muscles had quit taking orders from his brain as his body shut down.

"Go home, Compass."

Silas knew his friend had already departed, but Red's demand echoed in the silent realm of chaos surrounding him, driving him to regroup.

"Your place was always on the ranch." The twins peered over Seth's shoulder as his brothers tried to grant him the strength to move.

"Yes, come back to us, Si."

"Lucy?" What was she doing here? On the rig? He had to get her out. Silas scrambled on awkward elbows and his working knee, ignoring the slices he gouged into his joints as he slithered toward the ghost of her in that gauzy sundress he'd been enchanted by as a kid.

"I've missed you, Silas." Colby had one arm around Lucy's waist and the other extended to him in invitation. Why weren't they running?

Silas tumbled down the stairs then made one final lunge, trying to shield his loved ones. His arms flailed through the mirage.

Alluring ghosts.

A fantasy.

Grateful for their safety, he recoiled at losing them again.

He attempted a half-hearted pounce for the platform he'd somehow reached. A tertiary explosion had projectiles pinging off surfaces all around him. It took him a few seconds to realize the pain lancing his body meant he'd stopped at least some of the macabre confetti with his flesh.

He started to cover his mouth—the gasses entering when he gulped stung his lungs—but a chunk of metal stuck in his palm. Odd, he couldn't feel it anymore.

One final reverberation, larger than the ones before, tossed him into the corner like a rag doll. The sick crunch of his ribs guaranteed he'd broken one or two at least.

The fringes of his vision dimmed.

As darkness claimed him, he saw his parents, his brothers, Lucy, Colby and even Buddy—his childhood dog—waiting on Compass Ranch. When they welcomed him with open arms, he accepted that he'd died and gone to heaven.

All he could think was that he didn't deserve such an honor.

# Chapter Three

"Colby! JD!"

Lucy didn't give a damn if she spooked every animal on the ranch. The screen door to the main house slammed behind her. She screamed for her husband again as she tore along the porch and crossed the yard, past the freshly painted barn.

Ranch hands stared at the unusual display, several jogging after her to offer assistance. None of them would do.

In the distance, she caught a glimpse of the two men she sought astride gorgeous mounts. When she waved her arms but kept running, they spurred the horses to a gallop. It was silly. She couldn't reach them faster than they could ride back. Still, she didn't bother to stop herself from ducking between the rails of the fence to intercept them a millisecond sooner.

Thank God they hadn't left for the outer pastures yet.

On any other day she might have taken an instant to admire the two powerful men racing side by side—the owner of Compass Ranch and his foreman—as they barreled down on her. Right now, she needed the arms of her husband as she delivered terrible news.

The stuff of a parent's nightmares.

Colby started dismounting before his horse had come to a complete stop. He dropped beside her, cupping her shoulders in his broad hands to peer at her tear-stained face.

"What's the matter, Luce?" His sun-kissed cheeks appeared pale, an impressive feat. "What is it?"

He shook her a bit when the truth strangled her.

JD pried Colby's fingers from her arm then snuggled her into a paternal embrace. In the six years since her dad had suffered a massive heart attack and died while treating a foal in the middle of the night, JD had taken over as her honorary father. After raising four sons and countless ranchers, he got a mite protective over his little girl.

He smoothed her hair, shooting a glare at Colby after inspecting the red marks lingering on the skin bared by her tank top.

"Shit! Sorry." Her husband whipped his hat from his head and slapped it on his thigh. "You're killing me, baby. What's wrong?"

Lucy gulped, reaching for his hand. He cradled it this time, begging her with those sky blue eyes not to say their worst fear aloud. She couldn't give him what he hoped for.

"It's bad." She smothered another sob. "It's Si."

"Oh, Jesus."

"Is he..." Even tough-as-nails JD Compton couldn't finish the thought.

"He's alive, but seriously injured. There was some kind of explosion. He's been in the hospital for three weeks." Regret knotted her guts, making it almost impossible to continue. She drew one ragged breath, then another and another. "Twenty-three days. Suffering. Alone. With no one by his side when the doctors weren't sure he'd pull through."

Relief chased terror across the faces hovering

over her. She could relate. Her heart hadn't stopped stuttering since she'd taken the call from a concerned nurse who had the good sense to ignore Silas's idiotic request not to notify his family.

From one caregiver to another, Lucy could understand. Sometimes the patient couldn't determine the best course of treatment. She owed the woman big time.

"The fool broke his femur, three ribs, sustained countless lacerations, contusions and burns. Plus, he had one hell of a concussion. Internal bleeding and the damage to his lungs caused the most concern, though. He's had seven surgeries and they say he'll probably always walk with a limp."

Anger had replaced the initial horror swamping her as the woman in the Anchorage hospital relayed the extensive list of Silas's injuries. How dare he keep his family ignorant when he needed them? She'd had enough of his arrogance. What gave him the right to steal other people's choices?

The girl she'd been might have been bowed beneath his heavy-handed ruling.

The woman she'd grown into certainly would not.

"The oil company is recognizing him as a hero. They say he saved hundreds of lives when their safety equipment failed." She glanced between JD and Colby.

She'd shared the brief phone conversation she'd had with Silas's roommate a couple months ago. She hadn't been able to stand the silence when he'd stopped emailing his brothers for two weeks, cutting off her information pipeline. The guys had tried to reach out to Silas when she pestered them. None of the three had gotten a response.

So she'd broken down and dialed, expecting to hang up on Silas's terse greeting like usual. Instead, the unfamiliar man on the other end of the line had startled her into making a betraying gasp. She'd begged him not to tell Silas she'd called. After he'd agreed, she couldn't help prying, just a little.

Silas had picked up extra shifts. No biggie there. She'd wondered if he had finally moved on when the sweet man on the other end of the line appreciated her genuine concern and expressed curiosity about Silas's history. Lucy had given him enough to help him understand the situation. It had hurt, but she'd hoped Silas could find some measure of happiness. In fact, she hadn't worried when he dropped off the grid this time because she assumed his obvious lover had kept him too busy for correspondence.

The poor man. "Red Covington died in the blast."

JD made the sign of the cross.

Colby swept her into his arms, surrounding her with his gentle warmth and reliable shelter. God, how she loved this man. So much, she accepted that she could lose him when Silas came home.

Tomorrow.

After a decade of exile, Prince Silas would return to his kingdom. Colby might still be under his spell. Denying her own infatuation would be pointless, though she wasn't the one in danger of being captured.

The passionate exchange she'd interrupted between Colby and Silas had fueled her best dreams and worst night terrors for ten long years. Never far from her mind, she remembered it often. How it had boiled her blood and frozen her heart.

The two men she craved wanted each other.

Not her.

Despite her naïve attempts at seduction, both men had kept her at arm's length. Colby had held her hand, kissed her sweetly and melted her heart but neither had shown her the raw lust she'd discovered they were capable of. At least not then. After Silas left, Colby had gradually warmed. She had no complaints about their love life but neither had he shown her that abandonment to raw obsession again.

Only one person had inspired that in him.

"They're sending Silas home. I arranged the flight with the hospital. Judy agreed to take over three of my homecare patients to clear time in my daily schedule. They're releasing him into my care." She cupped Colby's jaw with her trembling fingers. Could he read her understanding? His enduring desire for the other man didn't make her prize him less. No, even more, because he'd remained faithful to her all this time when she couldn't give him everything he needed, no matter how badly she wished she could. "Our care."

"Silas is coming home?" Colby sounded like she felt. Dazed. Excited. Terrified.

"Silas is coming home." JD whooped then hugged them both, a solid arm around each of them. "Things are gonna work out. The way they always should have been. You'll see."

Colby watched his wife jog to the house. She'd left Silas's mom, Victoria, inside. The woman had probably already rung half the state to arrange all they'd need to bring her eldest son home.

Colby distracted himself from worrying about the man he'd called his best friend once by studying Lucy's fine ass in those snug jeans, the curves highlighted by her soft pink shirt and the wild mass of her untamed hair. He adored those fiery curls, especially when they fanned over his chest each night as they fell asleep together.

She issued a watery smile over her shoulder before ducking inside. The quiet desperation thinning her lips made his stomach do flip-flops.

"What the hell are you going to do now, boy?"

"Don't have a fucking clue. Go on as usual, I suppose." Like anything could be normal with Silas at Compass Ranch again.

"Your wife is in love with my son. Has been since she was no higher than my knee."

"You think that's news to me, JD?"

"And what about you? Gonna admit you want Silas too?"

Colby spun on the heel of his boot, forcing himself to close his gaping mouth with a snap. He couldn't say what surprised him more, that JD knew or that he didn't seem too upset by the idea. No point in pretending things might have changed. What he carried for Silas couldn't be obliterated by time or distance.

"It don't matter. I'm married. Happily. I won't fuck around on Lucy. Si never wanted me anyway. Not with the fire he'd get in his eyes every time he saw Lu."

"No man's a good judge of shit that close to his heart. What seems obvious to others gets distorted, like the horizon on a hot day, when you're twisted up with need and devotion."

"Then why—?"

"I don't have all the answers, Colby. And I'm not trying to bust your balls either, just talking. This next bit will be rough for us all. More so for you. Make sure you're ready to grab the bull by its horns and sit tight. I have faith you'll tough it out. Hell, you're the only one of my sons that stuck. Every other one couldn't put up with this life. Took off the second they turned eighteen."

"They're morons. Every one of the Compass Brothers. I wouldn't have picked anyone else to be my father. No other place to call home." Pride at the man's compliment filled him with awe and gratitude. JD put his sons above all else. To be counted among them meant something. Something huge.

They pivoted as if by mutual agreement, standing shoulder to shoulder against the rail so they didn't have to look into each other's eyes. "You and Victoria raised your kids right. Nothing like my shithead sperm donor."

JD grunted his agreement.

Colby had always suspected it'd been the head of Compass Ranch who'd kicked the living crap out of his father to encourage the asshole to leave town. The sick bastard had limped from Compton Pass, never to be seen again, abandoning his teenage son. An hour later Vicky had showed up to claim the malnourished, beaten kid Colby had been and welcomed him into their lives. She'd tamed him like a wild animal, inching closer until he finally believed in the reality of their generosity, kindness and love.

The Comptons had given him shelter, a job and so much more. Family. A home.

A life worth living.

"I'm not planning on leaving Compass Ranch anytime soon if that's what you're working toward. I would never abandon you or Vicky or Lucy. Not after what Silas put you all through. I'll give him a chance to heal up, but we're gonna have words about it. That I promise."

Another long silence followed, this one easier as the firm set of JD's shoulders relaxed a hair. As they often did while catching a break, they shared the silence, watching over the ranch as they kept their own company.

Colby had become fast friends with all four Compass brothers—as the locals referred to them—overnight. Still, there'd always been something about Silas and Lucy. The three of them would take off on adventures, exploring the land and the bond growing between them.

Until things had spiraled out of control.

"Remember Jack Newton?"

Colby searched the recesses of his memory at JD's random interjection. A lot of wandering men had worked the ranch a summer or two but…Jack?

"Tall, skinny like a bean pole, mean as a bear with a tooth ache?"

"Ah, yeah. I remember that fucker. Never did trust him." More like he'd hated the way the man had appraised him with lurid intentions blatant in his stare.

"When I fired his ass, he tried to throw it in my face how he'd seen you and my 'fag son' going at it in the barn. How little Lucy caught you and bolted the night before Silas hightailed it out of here."

"Son of a bitch." Colby crashed his fist into the rough-hewn rail, regretting it as a spike of sensation traveled through his knuckles. "I fucked up, JD. Shit, I'm sorry. All these years. It's my fault he left. You knew, and you didn't kick me out?"

"Don't go getting stupider than you've already been, son."

"What's that supposed to mean?" He shook the sting from his hand.

"You three kids have been pissing away time like it goes on forever." JD rubbed his side, a gesture Colby had spied him making a few times lately. "Quit screwing around and set things straight. Whatever it takes. You're only given so long around this place. Use it well."

A million other questions tumbled through Colby's mind, but by the time he recovered, JD had already handed his horse to Jake—who worked the stable this morning—then headed inside to his wife. Despite Vicky's spine of steel, she probably wished for her husband at her side. Colby hoped his marriage, and Lucy's attachment to him, was half as strong as the extraordinary relationship JD had forged with his woman.

Anything less would make the fledgling plans kicking around in his brain unravel in a heartbeat. Phase one entailed corralling Lucy alone. Isolated from the herd of folks gathering on the front porch bearing pies, and hoping for extra gossip, as the news spread.

Less than a half hour had passed since their lives flipped inside out yet several pickups already cluttered the yard. The drone of more engines approaching along the winding drive from the main road, a few miles in the distance, insured extra casseroles and gossip headed this direction.

Colby should have realized the flaw in his plan when he had to stop twice on the way to the house. "Is there anything I can do?" Cindi, the cute bookkeeper who worked from a little office in the barn, stepped in front of him, swiping a stray lock of hair beneath the pencil wound in her hair.

"How about putting together a list of supplies from Lucy? She might need equipment we don't have here and can't find in town."

"Good idea. I have it covered. We're expecting a shipment tomorrow morning from Laramie. I'll make sure anything else comes with it."

"Great, thanks." He accepted her hug but didn't make it more than ten feet before he bumped into Leah Hollister.

"Whoa." Colby snagged the covered dish about to smash on the rocky yard.

"Nice catch, foreman." Compton Pass's sweet kindergarten teacher reclaimed the dish with a sad smile. She refused to let him help her carry it, always trying to prove herself. Someday he'd ask her why that was. "Are you hanging in?"

"Yeah. Need to find Lucy, though." He kept one hand on her elbow as they climbed the stairs. Such a tiny thing couldn't possibly see where she stepped around the comfort food she'd carted over in record time. How the hell did women do that?

"I think you missed her. She ran past while you were talking to Cindi. Said she was headed to the storage shed to dig out a few of Silas's things." The door opened before they reached it. Someone piled Leah's offering with the rest. The crowd swallowed her before he could slip another word in edgewise. He tried to break out, follow Lucy. No use. Someone else interrupted. Damn!

And so it went.

Despite valiant attempts, he didn't manage to isolate his wife until after midnight. All day, prying eyes and pointed comments had eroded his confidence. Lucy's infatuation with Silas had been no secret growing up. The entire community wondered what would happen if the chemistry zinged between her and Silas when the pair reunited at last.

Colby most of all.

What if she only wanted Si? Nothing—no one— more?

It had damn near killed Colby not to chase after Silas and beg him to come home. Survival without both halves of his soul would prove impossible. Only Lucy had made Silas's abandonment bearable.

Sometime in the last couple minutes his wife had sunk onto the floral-patterned sofa in Vicky's parlor and crashed. He studied her even breathing across the bar that opened into the family room of the ranch house while he finished drying glasses.

"I can clear these up." Vicky reached up to pat his back.

"I've got them." He smiled over his shoulder but couldn't hold her assessing gaze for more than a moment. "Almost done."

"If you squeeze a little harder you'll shatter it. I'm fond of that pattern." She *tsked* then applied pressure on the bunched muscles of his forearm until he paused. "Things will be all right."

He set the final cup on the counter then absorbed Vicky's hug. She didn't hound him to speak. Instead, she hung on until some of the tension seeped from him.

"There, that's better. Now, take that girl of yours home. She's exhausted herself."

"I can't believe she got Silas's old room ready so fast."

"That isn't what wore her out." Vicky stared at him as though he were slow. "Enough hiding, Colby. JD promised he spoke with you this morning. Maybe he didn't do a good enough job?"

"It's not fair for you two to gang up on me." He laughed then kissed her cheek. "JD did fine. It's just…"

"What?"

"It's been so long. If Si had taken her immediately maybe it would've been different. I wouldn't have known what I was missing. If I lose her to him now, I'll never survive it. But I want them to be happy. Both of them."

"So I guess you'll have to make sure all three of you win now, won't you?" She squeezed Colby as though she weren't condoning an illicit arrangement for her own son.

"How did you guess what I was thinking?"

She withdrew a fraction of an inch, one brow raised. "Why do men always think they're so subtle when they're after something?"

"You're okay with…?" He didn't how to describe the relationship he had in mind. He needed the three of them to be together, equals bonded permanently.

"It's called a triad, Colby." She chuckled when a blush heated his cheeks. "Plenty of people enjoy ménage. Shoot, in our day, JD and I—"

He choked. Christ, what was he, thirteen again?

"Yeah, well, you get the point." She grinned, relishing his discomfort a moment more before turning serious. "What's in your heart? Don't listen to anything else. A hell of a lot of people objected to JD and me when we first started dating."

"Why?" His head tilted as he absorbed the sincerity of her statement. He couldn't imagine two people better suited. What could society have possibly objected to?

"'Cause I was so young. He was handsome as sin, wealthy and nearly twenty years my senior. People couldn't believe affection or tenderness was involved." She grinned. "And he had quite a reputation for having a dark edge in bed."

"Okay, enough!" He didn't need to picture JD's dominant personality translating to sex. It reminded him too much of his dreams of Silas. He shook his head. "It's funny, I don't see any of that when I look at the two of you. I can't imagine either of you with anyone else."

"Exactly, Colby." She patted his cheek then nodded. "Folks might gawk or run their fool mouths at first. In time everyone else will accept you. I can't picture the three of you any other way."

"He's been gone so long." He wished he could kick his own ass when his whisper caused his surrogate mother to wince and the sheen of tears glistened in her eyes. "What if things are different?"

"If I know my boy at all, he'll be the same as ever. Headstrong, noble and hard-working." Vicky nibbled her lip as if debating whether to speak her mind. He waited her out, glad when she continued. "You needed this time, Colby. To grow into your own without Silas here. I think if he'd stayed, you never would have become so independent. You're a man to be proud of, honey. You earned your position as foreman and the other hands respect you. Lucy adores you. JD and I are lucky to have you. Silas would be too."

"Thank you." He hated the sting behind his scrunched eyelids.

"Now put your wife to bed right. She'll need her energy tomorrow."

"Yes, ma'am." He grinned as he rounded the bar and scooped Lucy into his arms.

She snuggled close to his chest and sighed, a perfect fit for his hold.

# Chapter Four

Lucy blinked at the hairline crack snaking across the plastered ceiling above her and Colby's bed. How had she gotten here?

The foreman's lodge lay half a mile east of the main house. She didn't remember the trip home. They certainly hadn't raced their mounts along the well-used trail as they did when they couldn't wait to crash into bed—or onto the kitchen floor—together. Neither did she recall driving herself in her Jeep as she did when she returned from a long day of tending to her elderly or terminal homebound patients.

It would have been impossible to forget riding double with Colby in the moonlight and crisp air as they did on occasion to relax after a long day. The security of her husband's muscled arm around her waist, his powerful thighs bracketing hers and the promise of his hard cock in the small of her back always had her eager for attention by the time they walked his gelding—Couper—bareback out of the farmyard, never mind along the entire trail to their house.

Sometimes they had to stop along the route.

She smiled to herself as she realized Colby must have driven her home sometime after she'd surrendered, promising to take a miniscule five-minute break before washing the mountain of dishes that had piled up. Nearly the entire town of Compton Pass had swung by the ranch at some point to show their support. The whole day melted into one long blur of activity.

The brush of supple cotton sheets on her breasts as she lay naked confirmed Colby had tucked her in. Undressing her infatuated him. He'd peel her clothes off as though he performed a sacred ritual intended to worship her body. The man treated her like a goddess.

Running water caught her attention. She rolled to her side and checked the clock on her nightstand. Nearly two in the morning. She considered joining her husband in the shower as he soaped his ripped muscles, honed by daily manual labor.

Every ridge and line would gleam beneath the slick suds.

Memories of many shared washings had her humming her approval. Despite the stress of the day, she couldn't shake the low level buzz that had haunted her since the news of Silas's homecoming. Her thighs parted a bit, and she ran one palm low on her abdomen. Engrossed in the recollection, she didn't notice Colby had finished until he strolled into their room.

"What's going on out here, naughty girl? Can't leave you alone for a minute." The twinkle in his eyes as he emerged with a towel slung low on his trim hips proclaimed he'd caught her thinking of him. With one glance, he read everything she felt. Exactly what she needed.

He ruffled the terrycloth over his damp hair, granting her a world-class view of grade A beefcake.

"Like what you see, Mrs. Peterson?"

"Mmm. You're one mighty fine cowboy."

A glimmer of doubt crossed her husband's face. "Was it me you were thinking of?"

Lucy levered onto her elbows, the sheet pooling at her waist. Things were serious when her bare breasts couldn't distract Colby. He had a thing for her tits, especially when her nipples stood straight out as they did now. He would spend hours ravishing the sensitive peaks.

He didn't glance away from her stare. His throat worked as he gulped. She patted the bedspread beside her hip, and he crossed to her in two moderate strides of his long legs.

"I *always* dream of you." She took a deep breath then admitted, "But sometimes you're not alone."

Her husband slid beneath the jewel box quilt Victoria had made for their wedding present, gathering Lucy to his chest. The pounding of his heart drummed in her ear.

"You truly believe I don't want you anymore, Colby?"

"For tonight, sure. Once Silas is home…" Her cheek rose and fell when he shrugged. "You've always loved him. Shit, you only agreed to date me in the first place to make him jealous."

"You knew that?"

"I'm not stupid, Lu. It pissed me off when he shunned your affection." He drew a deep breath. "Like he'd always done to me. Acting like we were nothing but friends. I understood how bad that would sting you."

"Colby, we were young." Her sigh buffeted his nipple, hardening the dime-sized point, stealing her attention for a moment.

"Especially you. I wondered if Silas kept his hands off because you hadn't even turned seventeen yet. But I couldn't resist. I never was as honorable as him."

"Don't say things like that." She lifted her head to

meet her husband's troubled stare. Her fingers stroked damp hair off his brow. "What I meant is that I was too inexperienced to comprehend all you had to offer. You're subtle where he's flash. You're steady where he's hot then cold. You're reliable, trustworthy and sexier than any man has a right to be."

"You're good for my ego, Lu."

"You're good for my soul."

When he dragged her close for a drugging kiss, she tasted the cherry candy he popped like mints when he worried. Didn't he understand?

"You were always spectacular and you've done a hell of a lot of growing since those days, Colby. No potential went to waste with you." She forced herself to put some distance between their torsos or she'd forget what she intended to say. Still, she couldn't stop herself from walking her fingertips up his chest, over the contours of his neck, to his lips. "I admire how you forged yourself into the man you are today. You didn't have all of Silas's advantages and yet you've become one of the most respectable leaders on the ranch and in Compton Pass. Hell, I heard rumors in town they're going to write you in on the ballet for trustee this year."

"Funny." He nipped her finger then sucked until the sting disappeared. "Victoria said something similar earlier. You didn't need any polish, Lu. You've always been perfect to me. Even when you schemed to use your pal Colby to make Si suffer."

"It didn't take long for me to realize I already had what I wanted." She leaned forward to taste his lips once more. No use in resisting. His palm landed on her ass, cupping her as they shared a deep, lingering kiss. She chuckled around his fluttering tongue then dislodged her mouth to whisper, "I think we dated all of one day before I begged you to take my virginity."

He'd refused.

She still couldn't say if it had been some misplaced sense of propriety or the fact that he'd lusted for someone else more than her. The sliver of doubt had niggled the far recesses of her mind for too long. Soon, she'd find out. Suddenly, she wasn't as eager for the answer. Her life here was perfect. She had everything important. Almost.

Colby bundled her into his arms then rolled onto his back, pillowing her on his gorgeous body. She rested their foreheads together until the creases that appeared on his brow when he discussed something serious crinkled against her skin.

"When we hooked up, you had s*ome* of what you wanted. Let's be honest, Lucy. You've always craved Silas. We both have."

The truth they'd tried to deny for so long reared between them. A tear leaked from her watering eyes without warning, dropping onto Colby's cheek.

"That doesn't mean I love you any less," she promised.

"Then you understand it's the same for me?"

She nodded. Ten years of Colby's easy companionship and generous passion didn't lie. Too bad Silas hadn't shown a glimmer of interest in her. When the object of her girlhood crush had clutched Colby to him, ravaging her then-boyfriend in the barn, the sight had sliced her in two. Jealousy had sickened her. She fled, praying she'd make it far enough that her ultimate disappointment wouldn't douse the sparks between the two men she adored.

Lucy hadn't done a good enough job of hiding her disappointment.

Silas had bolted the very next day, before she had a chance to guarantee him of her happiness for them. How much time had she stolen from Colby? From Silas? How callous did it make her that she'd savored her husband's devotion despite the cost?

She swore she'd set things straight and grant them the bliss she'd hoarded for a decade.

For one more night, her husband belonged to her alone.

"I'm not sure what tomorrow will bring, but if Silas is the same man we adored, you have to pursue your heart's desire Colby. For all of our sakes'." She couldn't bear to keep him from Si a moment longer. Colby would have chased the other man down long ago if it hadn't been for the responsibility he felt for her, the ranch and a million other real-life hurdles. "I won't be an obstacle to your happiness."

Her husband flipped her, rising over her supine form on straight-locked arms until he could peer into her eyes. She made sure only the hope for his bliss projected from them.

"Jesus, I'm crazy about you. I've stressed all day about how to tell you exactly the same thing, Lucy." He tangled his fingers in the curls at her temples and claimed her lips in ravenous kisses between vows. "I *will* fight for us. I promise. I'll do my best to convince him."

And then she'd be alone. No more sultry nights filled with familiar laughter and unending passion or the occasional disagreement resolved with gentle loving. Lucy reached for something to tide her through the lonely darkness to come.

A precious memory.

"Love me, Colby?"

"I'll always love you. No matter what comes tomorrow. Or the day after." He rubbed his nose against hers. "Or the day after that. I swear I'll never stop, Lu. I wouldn't have thought it possible, but I cherish you more for giving us this chance. For understanding."

Her heart broke. She nodded anyway. Us. Colby

and Silas. Despite what her husband claimed, he wouldn't be able to deny his lust. She didn't have to have psychic abilities to predict the future.

Colby didn't waste any time in displaying his gratitude. He laid a trail of wet kisses down her neck, across the tops of her breasts, through the valley between them, along her center to her pussy. His hands lit her nerve endings on fire as he caressed her in tandem. He teased the edge of her mound with glancing swipes of his fingers before settling in the cradle of her thighs.

Her husband sighed as he inhaled the scent of her arousal then laid his cheek on her mound as though to ground himself before continuing. She petted his damp hair then nudged him toward her aching core.

"So hot, Lu?" He grinned up at her, his irises the shocking blue they turned when his desire took control. "What if I feel like going slow?"

"Jackass. You don't."

"Damn straight." Colby scooped his hands beneath her ass then raised her to his mouth. He sipped from her moist folds, feeding on every molecule of her arousal.

Lucy's hips flexed in his hold, her body undulating of its own accord when he neared her clit with his roving lips.

"There." She buried her fingers in his hair to keep him still when he'd reached the perfect position. "Right there."

His smile spread against her slippery tissue. Of course he knew exactly how to touch her. He liked to tease, that's all. God, he made torturing her an art form.

Lucy shivered then smoothed the heels of her palms up her tummy to her breasts, planning to fight fire with fire. She cupped the soft swells in her hands, playing with her nipples using the tips of her fingers.

Colby paused his assault to stare. He groaned, vibrating her clit with his pleasure. When she winked at her husband, he slipped in some tricks of his own. One of his hands glided from her hip to her pussy. His broad middle finger nudged the opening, tracing her inner lips before delving inside.

Her hands fell to the mattress, her sweet torment abandoned. She slipped her legs from beneath his arms, propping her heels on his ridiculously wide shoulders. When her husband applied the perfect level of suction on her engorged bundle of nerves, her toes curled into his muscles.

"Ah!" She cried out when he added a second finger, stretching her pussy, preparing her for his cock. She couldn't decide if she'd prefer him to keep eating her or to fill her with his impressive length. Colby didn't ask. He pursued her nearing climax with a single-minded determination she found attractive both in and out of bed.

God help her when her man fixated on something. He'd go to the ends of the earth to make his desire reality.

His calloused finger massaged a hidden spot nestled deep in her body. He played her like a violin virtuoso with a Stradivarius. Lucy attempted to resist, to prolong Colby's seductive gift. When he added a third finger and rotated them all so he stimulated the clenching walls of her channel, she stood no chance.

Lucy slapped the mattress. The pressure building within her required an outlet. She squirmed and shouted nonsense her husband understood on an instinctive level far beyond decipherable language. He took pity on her, sucking her clit into his mouth as he spread his fingers apart, triggering a climax of epic proportions.

She hadn't yet finished coming when Colby covered her with his entire frame. Her legs wrapped around his trim hips, opening her pussy to invite him inside.

Her husband tunneled into her clinging sheath, joining their bodies as tightly as their spirits entwined. The fit of their flesh impressed her every time. Though she'd never had another man, she couldn't imagine a match as perfect as this.

What would it be like to hold Silas inside her instead?

"Yes. God, yes." Colby shuddered over her. "Do that again. Clench my cock."

She thought of the responsible, brave and daring young man she'd hungered for all her life then pictured the man he'd become. She closed her eyes and allowed her imagination to run wild. In her mind, he claimed possession of her, fucking her without the restraint her husband insisted on for her protection.

"That's it, Lu." Colby grunted as he shuttled in and out of her with urgent glides. The contracted ring of muscle at her entrance caught the ridge below the head of his cock on every pass, preventing him from abandoning her pussy despite his quickening thrusts.

She wished she could taste the fluid leaking from his cock as it always did when he came this close to shooting. The salty emission mingled with her copious lubrication to facilitate his amplified motion. Colby fucked her harder, dropping his mouth to hers, whispering his affection against her skin.

He kissed her with a tenderness the pounding of his hips should have belied. Urgency overwhelmed them both, guaranteeing his care, his concern and his soul-deep adoration. Because she returned the sentiment, her open heart allowed her to sense the slight imperfection in their joining.

Colby needed something else to achieve the rapture flooding her in wave after wave. Familiar regret threatened their harmony. She couldn't satisfy all of his desires. Still, she would do her best.

Lucy nipped her husband's lip to get his attention. When his driving rhythm hitched, she shoved his shoulders, urging him to turn. He complied with a moan, rotating until he flopped onto his back. His spread fingers trailed from her ribs to her hips, confirming she'd settled herself comfortably before setting her loose.

Her husband relinquished control, handing her the reins. She tipped back, supporting herself with her hands braced on his thighs to give him room to do her bidding. He licked his fingertip then played with her clit, eager to serve.

Lucy rode him with a variety of motions designed to drive him insane. She rocked her hips in a series of short bursts that concentrated her tightest muscles on the head of his cock before grinding onto him fully.

The jerk of his erection inside her corresponded to the curses spilling from his lips. "Fuck. Ah. Shit. Yes. Damn!"

Colby slammed his hips upward with each utterance, his climax triggering a second wash of ecstasy in Lucy. He never could resist when she took charge. Spurts of his come splattered on her swollen tissue, filling her with his thick, white cream.

She raised herself until he shot the last strand on the outside of her pussy. Before she could rub the opalescent fluid into her flesh, he tugged her hip, forcing her to straddle his head. He surprised her when he devoured the pearly concoction.

Would he be so eager to ingest Silas's come?

The thought rocketed her to an instant orgasm. She ground her pussy on her husband's wriggling tongue. Before she could process what had happened, he'd tucked her into his solid embrace—face to face—

so she could ride out the storm.

"Things are different already," he whispered into her hair. "That was…"

"Amazing." She panted, her breath impossible to catch.

"Wild." He massaged her relaxing muscles, sighing when she settled more fully against the contours of his body. "The same, but better."

"Exactly." Lucy couldn't stop touching her husband, petting every inch of exposed skin. "Scary."

"Why?" He cupped her cheek in his hand, tilting her face toward his.

"I'm afraid our relationship will never be the same."

"Only enhanced, Lu." His half-hard cock perked up when he communicated his optimism with a thorough kiss. "We'll never lose this."

They rocked together until the length of his erection firmed against her belly. He reached down and slipped inside her once more. They soothed each other with tender, lingering touches that focused on bonding rather than fucking for the sake of the prize at the end of the performance.

Lucy had never fathomed such an intimate exchange could exist. She couldn't say how long they held each other, hours maybe, before a gentle, reassuring warmth rained over her soul to match the heat flooding her womb. Ecstasy washed her clean of her troubles.

Colby stared into her eyes as he surrendered. The vocalization of their love became unnecessary as he communicated the value of their mating on a level far beyond words. She struggled to stay awake, to linger on the alternate plane they'd created with their exchange, but before she was ready, exhaustion and the security of his hold lulled her to sleep.

When she woke, Colby was gone.

# Chapter Five

Silas groaned. He attempted to roll over to relieve the discomfort in his side but a canvas strap around his waist pinned him to a gurney. Fuck! He'd objected to being shipped home like a hunk of meat. Doctors had overruled his arguments. Crowded Alaskan hospitals forced them to release him despite his protests.

Once the insurance company found out about Lucy and the exceptional level of homecare she'd offered to provide, they'd assumed he would be thrilled. When he'd fought instead, the doctors had subdued him with a shot of something strong.

So strong he didn't remember anything else until this moment. Probably for the best.

Voices swirled around his clouded mind. He couldn't quite make out what they were saying. Then a beam of light stabbed through an opening to his left, illuminating the interior of a tiny plane, and hot air buffeted his face. At least it seemed steamy to him.

Silas didn't have to wonder where in the world he lay or if this stop were a transfer en route because fresh air enveloped him like a comforting hug, easing the pain he'd endured for the past month. No, since he'd left this place. His heaven on earth.

The smell of home—fresh mountain air, late

summer flowers and hints of the cow pasture near the ranch's airfield—had him flaring his nostrils like a stallion scenting a mare in heat. He blinked and shook his head, struggling to stay awake. Ironic, considering all the times he'd battled the intrusion of his alarm to linger in a dream of Compass Ranch a moment or two longer.

He might have thought it another vision, or maybe heaven this time, when a familiar woman called to him. "Oh, Silas."

The backlighting of the hatch caused a blurry silhouette, haloed by Wyoming sunshine, to materialize above him. Thank God for the buckles locking his arms by his sides or he wouldn't have been able to prevent himself from groping forbidden fruit. The lure of his personal siren's proximity after years and miles of separation overwhelmed all his logic.

"Lucy." The gruff bark seemed indecipherable but she came closer, dropping to her knees beside him. His frustrated bellows, not to mention the sedation the Alaskan interns had forced on him, acted like nettles stuffed down his throat.

"Si." The ragged gasps of her breath betrayed her weeping, though he still couldn't see her clearly. "Look at you."

Gentle hands stroked his scruffy face, his chest and his arms, stealing his ability to speak. When she entwined their fingers and laid her head on his shoulder, whispering prayers of thanks for his safety over his heart, he stared at her gorgeous mane of curls. Some things never changed.

"Come on, sweetheart."

Silas tensed at the inherent command radiating from the latest form, highlighted by the sun. "Let's take him home. We'll catch up there."

"Colby?" It seemed some things did change. The

broad, filled-out form exuded power and a potent strength Silas didn't quite remember. Impressive. He hoped whatever blanket they'd covered him with for the trip hid the erection struggling to form despite the drugs lingering in his system.

His gut clenched, and he closed his eyes. Leaving had been the smart decision. He never could have controlled himself around these two. Reports of home from his brothers and his parents confirmed the couple's lasting happiness. He had no business intruding.

Colby crouched near his wife, one hand rubbing her back with an ease that made it clear he'd done it a million times before. Silas had never built familiarity with a partner. Other than Red, he'd forbidden repeat performances. His chest ached with regret.

For his friend.

For himself.

What would it be like to have that kind of unconditional support? He'd flown solo long enough to forget.

The tiny space grew cramped to the max when the weight of another passenger rocked the aircraft. This set of shoulders blocked the sun entirely. Lucy, Colby and JD came into view, the sight so overwhelming it almost knocked him out again. He swam toward the sunshine, the heat and the people he treasured. He couldn't bear to depart again so soon.

"Welcome home, son."

Surely, the rasp in his father's greeting had to do with his aging and not unbridled emotion. Right?

"JD." He couldn't say more but didn't have to. Three sets of hands braced him now, promising to lend him strength.

"Rest. We've got you," JD reassured him. "You'll need all your energy when your mama sees you. Prepare yourself. She's likely to squeeze you in half...or beat your ass with a wooden spoon. It's kind of a toss-up at this point."

Silas laughed, or tried to. The pain in his side dimmed his vision.

No! He scrambled toward the shimmering light but couldn't gain a firm toehold on consciousness. He spiraled into nothingness, everything in him straining to rejoin his family.

Lucy sat in the corner of the room, watching Victoria alternate sobs with shouts at her stubborn son, who occupied the king-sized bed in the center of his boyhood room. Colby stood by Lucy's side, his supportive grip on her shoulder helping to keep her relaxed.

Well, as much as she could be.

She'd anticipated that the jolt of desire Silas had always inspired in her would rear between them when they connected once more. And it had. But the intensity of the reaction had surprised her. It flared a hundred times brighter than the naïve infatuation she'd experienced as a young girl.

The injuries dotting his body, draining his alertness, had stopped her from mounting him where he lay. The wounds evident in his tortured gaze had broken her heart. She shivered as she remembered the undisguised agony she'd spotted in his dazed stare.

"Want me to find your sweater?" Colby whispered near her ear.

"No thanks." She capitalized on his nearness, stealing a kiss, needing the fortification to gel her insides, which threatened to dissolve into a pile of mush.

"He's going to be okay." Her husband sipped from her lips again.

"Are *we*?" She shivered again. "Did you feel it? The connection..."

"Did I?" Colby breathed hard though she doubted their kisses inspired his elevated respiration. "I still do."

Lucy couldn't help herself. She glanced at the crotch of her husband's ripped work jeans, sighing when she spotted the bulge there.

"Behave." He rearranged himself. The gesture didn't obscure the evidence. "I'm trying not to be obvious here, but it won't quit."

"Want me to take care of you?" Lucy squirmed in the chair. It'd been three hours since Silas had crashed into their lives again and already she thought she might die if someone didn't touch her soon. "I'll meet you in the bathroom downstairs in five minutes. I bet Vicky's good for another half hour of lecturing."

"At least." Colby winced.

They'd all faced the mama bear's wrath once or twice, but even the time Sawyer had gotten caught stealing from the general store for the hell of it his junior year of high school had generated less stern disappointment than this.

"When you have problems, you don't run from family. You *trust* the people who love you. I did not raise you to shirk your responsibilities. Your place was here. Always here. Not like your brothers, who dreamed of something else. What made you think the answer was lying to us? To yourself? To Colby and Lucy?"

"I feel kind of bad abandoning him. Especially for a BJ. Even one of yours, baby." Her husband hunched his shoulders and jammed his hands in his pockets when Vicky aimed her laser vision at him. He froze—like a deer in the headlights—until she turned back to her eldest son, disaster averted.

"...disrespectful..."

Lucy peeked up at Colby and grinned. Someday she hoped to have half as much command over her men and their children.

*Men?*

Oh damn, when had she gotten so greedy? Could it really be possible to keep them both? She had to try at least.

"...wasteful..."

Something about the energy surrounding the three of them when they'd touched in the ranch's plane, which they'd rigged to haul their damaged friend home from Cheyenne, had electrified her. Given her hope.

"...unhealthy..."

Lucy grimaced at the rising pitch of Vicky's diatribe. She thought she could hear dogs howling in the yard. When she shifted to leave the room, regardless of the danger from Silas's mom, the tirade stopped short.

"And I love you more than I can say. I missed you, Silas." Vicky smothered her son in hug tight enough to break another rib or two. "Please, don't ever do that to us, or yourself, again. This accident is a blessing in disguise. It's brought you home, where you belong."

"Is this still my place?" Silas broke his silence.

"Absolutely." Vicky answered before either Colby or Lucy could interject.

"How do you know?" Their injured friend fiddled with the edge of the blanket covering him.

"Because I'm your mother." She kissed his forehead then glanced toward the corner where Lucy and Colby waited. "You can still set things to rights. Be true to yourself. Make me proud, Silas."

"I'm working on it." He sighed. "I don't blame you for not believing me, but it's what I always tried to do."

"Foolish boy." Her warm tone betrayed the true feelings behind her criticism. "Don't struggle so hard. The solution is easy if you let it be. Listen to your heart."

Vicky rested her palm on her son's bare chest before nodding then leaving the room, shutting the door behind her.

No one moved.

No one spoke.

Lucy couldn't swear she breathed.

Colby acted first. He pried her white-knuckled fingers from the arms of her chair then helped her stand. Together they walked, side by side, toward the bed. Toward Silas.

The puffy slashes of fresh scars marring his skin threatened to distract her. He seemed so pale. Whether his injuries or his time hidden from the sun had leeched his color she couldn't tell. It made him appear cold. So did his tight nipples, which stood proud above the line of the sheet. The bright cotton cover obscured the lower half of his body from her wandering gaze.

He hadn't shaved in forever. The scruffiness worked for him. Still, she couldn't wait for him to reveal his strong jaw and the other hints of masculinity he'd grown into well.

"Christ, you're so beautiful. More than I guessed, Lu."

When his compliment knocked her off balance, he covered the gap.

"Are you going to yell at me too?" The mischievous grin she recognized from their childhood made an appearance even if it seemed a little rusty.

"Not exactly what I had in mind." Colby answered for them both. He scrubbed his hands through his sun-bleached hair then cursed. "Hell if I know where to go from here, though."

Lucy opened her mouth to make a suggestion. Silas interrupted. "Can I ask you something first?"

She nodded.

"Are you happy, Lu?" He tilted his head when her eyes narrowed. "I mean, really happy. And Colby too. Please promise me those lonely nights were worth it."

"Jesus, dickhead." Colby filled in when no sound would pass the knot in her throat. "Did you listen to one word Vicky said?"

"Yeah, she told me to follow my heart." Silas's rugged face, stressed by years of hard living—and, if she wasn't mistaken, dented by the subtle unevenness caused by patches of frostbite—expressed his genuine interest. "All it's ever wanted was to protect you. Both of you. To preserve your happiness."

Lucy exchanged a look with her husband, enough to convey more than an entire conversation between most people. Colby nodded.

"Clearly, you didn't read a single one of my letters." Lucy plopped onto the mattress when her knees buckled. "Wow, that's probably a solid three months of my life wasted."

Maybe they'd deluded themselves all this time. Had Silas departed without a glance over his shoulder? Had his nobility supplied a convenient excuse? She scooted toward the edge, prepared to leave and reevaluate the situation, when his hand braceleted her wrist.

His hold sent electricity through her core.

"I couldn't." He coughed after the rush of air he'd expelled, his lungs still not fully recovered. When the fit extended, Silas's face flushing an unhealthy shade of purple, she reached for the pitcher of water beside the bed.

Colby wrapped his arm around Silas's shoulders

then tipped their lost friend forward until she could touch the cup she held to his lips. He didn't drink for a moment, as though his pride rebelled at needing help to accomplish something so simple. Eventually, he accepted her offering.

The cool liquid soothed Silas. Lucy expected her husband to lower the man to the mountain of pillows arranged behind him. Instead, he stared at the expanse of their friend's back.

"You should see this, Lu."

"Does he have more cuts and burns there?" She nibbled her lip. Nurses couldn't be squeamish. She usually wasn't, but the extensive damage Silas had sustained wrung her stomach. "Should I grab some fresh bandages?"

"Yeah, he's pretty tore up. That's not what I'm talking about, though."

Silas met her gaze. He stared, offering no input. Close enough to kiss him, she watched him lick the last of the water droplets from his cracked lips. She opened a tube of balm she'd laid by the bed, part of her standard patient kit, and swirled some onto her finger. She'd applied the silky gel to many people in her career. None of them had made it seem like a dirty act. Tracing Silas's parted mouth inspired her to flush then avert her eyes.

They weren't ready yet.

Lucy forced herself to retreat, at least far enough to carefully straddle him as she crossed to his other side. Examining him from beneath Colby's supportive hold would prove impossible. She gasped when something hard and long brushed her thigh. "You're supposed to be sick."

"I'd have to be dead not to get a rise in my Levi's with you in my lap."

"Amen." Colby chuckled from where he kept

Silas upright. "Except you're not wearing any pants, big guy. There's some serious crackage happening back here."

"I think I'm skipping down the yellow brick road in Oz about now. It looks like I'm on Compass Ranch, but I really cracked my skull in that explosion and I'm lying on the rig while the world burns around me."

"God, Si." Lucy couldn't stop herself from hugging him. She wrapped herself lightly around his torso and visualized absorbing his pain. Her touch seemed to break him from the memories assaulting him, at least long enough for him to make a joke.

"Any minute now flying monkeys are going to zoom past that fucking window. Keep the crazy lady on the bike away from me, okay? She gives me the willies."

"Is it impossible to believe you're home?" Lucy stroked his fuzzy cheek.

"It's either that or you're all insane. Most husbands wouldn't find it amusing when some random guy wants to fuck his wife."

"I'm not most husbands. And you're not any guy."

"That probably makes this worse." Silas arched his hips, grinding himself against Lucy's mound. She thought she might come on the spot. He desired her!

Relief poised her on the verge of tears and had naughty ideas screaming for attention.

Lucy scrambled to the other side of her patient before she landed them all in trouble. If he needed medical attention, that had to come first. They could figure out the rest later. It was enough that attraction zinged through him too.

When she spied what her husband stared at, she gasped. "Oh, my God."

"Is it ruined?" Silas's frame heaved with the

disappointment he couldn't suppress, shifting the image decorating his strong flesh. "Is Snake still around? Maybe he can fix it up for me."

"Hell, no. I mean, Snake's still kicking but..." Colby murmured reverently, "it's fucking great. Perfect. I wish I'd thought of it."

Lucy couldn't stop herself. She traced the compass spanning his shoulders with her index finger. "It's crazy, Si. There are slices, yellowed bruises, half-healed blisters and scrapes all around it. But nothing touched the tattoo. Not one single thing harmed it."

"Maybe Mom is right."

"Isn't she always?" Colby ducked down for a better look. "What is that, there, between the cattle brand and the barn? I see something in the shadows."

"No one's ever noticed before." Silas groaned. "Not even my brothers."

"It's your name, Colby." Lucy bent forward to kiss the patch of skin, honoring the bond that had driven Si to carry her husband with him always. She'd known the instant she witnessed their embrace in the barn, they were meant for each other.

"Holy crap. You're right. It is." Colby's shock might have been funny if the significance of the moment didn't ripple through their entire lives. "And yours."

"What?" She followed the direction of her husband's pointing finger. Then she saw it. The tail of the y in her name entwined with the o in Colby.

Her hand flew to her mouth. Her knuckles couldn't stifle her sob.

"Now you did it, Si. You made our girl cry." He settled the injured man against the pillows, allowing both guys to peer into her unfocused eyes.

Lucy touched her cheeks with trembling fingers. Sure enough, tears dampened the skin there. She couldn't resist them any longer.

When she held her arms out to Colby, he lifted her over Silas's torso, into his arms. Instead of burrowing into his chest as she usually did on the rare occasions she succumbed to the need for a good cry, she kissed his jaw then turned. Careful not to hurt Silas, she tucked beneath his left arm and rested her cheek on his chest.

He stiffened beneath her for a few seconds before her tears melted his rigid hold.

"Shh, Lu." He petted her hair with awkward pats. "Please, it destroys me when you're upset."

She couldn't stem the flood now that it had started. In the periphery of her blurry vision, she caught him shooting Colby a plea for help. Her husband knew how to comfort her. He lowered himself to the mattress behind her, snuggling up tight to whisper soothing nonsense in her ear while he bracketed her with warmth.

Silas curled his arm around them both, his grip faint yet discernable.

"I'm sorry, Lucy." His voice weakened, as though her misery sapped his strength. His agony increased the flow of her tears. She cried for all the nights they'd spent apart. For all the times he'd had no one to lean on. For so many wasted years.

"Do you have any concept of what you're apologizing for?" Colby sounded kind of pissed. She couldn't catch her breath long enough to referee.

"Not really." Silas went slack beneath her. "Anything that causes her pain. Everything I've ever done. All the stuff I've fucked up. For all three of us..."

He whispered the last.

"If you hadn't trashed her letters maybe you would have figured it out sooner. She told you every fucking day. How much she missed you. How much we needed you. The gaping hole you left behind never closed up. Never healed over." Colby found the strength to say what she couldn't. Not again. "She told you over and over that we care for you, and that we'd always be here, waiting for you to come home. You bastard."

Silas shivered beneath her.

"Kept them. Every one. In my duffle, have them all. Waited for them. Collected them. Slept with one under my pillow. Couldn't read them. Couldn't stand to hear about the one place I ached to be and could never go," Silas murmured, on the verge of losing consciousness again. It'd been a long day, full of stress and sedatives strong enough to knock out a horse. "I never stopped loving you either. Promise."

Silas's confession and the running stream of Lucy's tears consumed the last of his stamina. He faded into a restless sleep beneath her cheek. For a long time, she clung to the man she'd lost while the one who'd caught her did it again. The three of them stayed like that.

Together.

All night long.

Silas picked at the knot in the tattered ribbon securing the bundle of letters he'd received in the first six months he spent in Alaska. After Lucy had departed for the day to tend her other patients, amidst a slew of unnecessary apologies, Colby had set the bricks of correspondence on the tray at Silas's side then unplugged the TV in his room.

"You can stare at the wall all day, or you can read those."

How fucking demented did it make Silas that Colby's iron will turned him on? The innate authority his friend possessed made the prospect of topping the man that much more alluring. He'd give every penny of the wages he'd hoarded for the past decade to bend Colby over the edge of the bed and screw him senseless.

He could make the foreman enjoy it.

Beg for more.

Caught in the daydream of burying himself repeatedly in Colby's tight heat, penetrating the ass he suspected had never welcomed a stiff cock, he tuned out the rest of the frustrated man's rant until Colby grabbed his hair as though he might attempt to tug it out. Silas blinked, dissolving the lurid movie playing in his imagination. Torn between admitting his depravity and letting his friend assume he'd ignored him on purpose, Silas hesitated too long.

Colby started to say something but closed his mouth, opened it again then spun on the heel of his boot. He reappeared in the doorway long enough to toss a cordless phone onto the bed. "Lucy's one, I'm two and JD is three on speed dial. Your mom will be back from her lunch with Lydia Redmond in an hour or so. Sometimes they like to shop afterward, though I doubt she will today."

Colby clomped down the stairs and onto the front porch. The screen door slammed behind him. Good thing Vicky hadn't heard it. She'd have ripped him a new one, foreman or not.

Silas tried to doze, but the sweet oblivion of sleep eluded him. Hell, he'd spent most of the past month unconscious. His body healed exponentially now, fueling his impatience to be up and about again. Especially with the lure of Compass Ranch right outside these prison walls.

He idled another quarter hour testing the strength in his leg.

He'd managed to convince himself he might be

able to stand without the crutches propped near the door, ten feet from his resting place, until he twisted something funny and delivered a bolt of agony up his spine. The resulting jerk of his torso tweaked his ribs. Sweating, cursing and grumbling, he resettled himself on the pillows. He couldn't achieve the level of comfort Lucy had provided when she'd tended him.

In an act of desperation, he stared at his laptop, willing the hunk of plastic and metal to levitate to the bed from the desk as though he'd mastered the Jedi mind trick.

No such luck.

The yellowed paper of Lucy's letters scared the shit out of him and tempted him at the same time. Sort of like the woman who'd authored them. He trailed the tip of one finger over their edges, noting the dulled corners on most from his frequent handling.

If he were honest, he'd admit he'd never opened them because he would have run straight home if she'd given him the slightest bit of hope. How stupid had he been all those years? What had really frightened him?

Would he continue on as he had, or find the courage to do better? Suddenly, it seemed as though the only person with a problem accepting the truth was him.

"Son of a bitch." Silas worked the knot until the faded satin unraveled. He plucked the first letter from the stack and slid his finger beneath the flap on the back. With one motion, he shredded the seal along the top then withdrew the lined paper from within.

Lucy's elegant script flowed over page after page.

*Dear Silas,*

*I can't say how many times I've written that salutation yet never before have I meant it so sincerely. Today is the first day Compass Ranch is without you and the absence is horrifyingly apparent. Colby and Seth took your place, covering your chores and their own. Colby even made your run to town with the extra chicken eggs for the farmer's market since it's Tuesday.*

*I thought Sam and Sawyer might want a cut of the responsibility, but the twins don't seem to share the same love for this life as we do. For Colby, it's a golden opportunity. I can see how it might be more of a burden on your brothers. At least now. They're young and eager for freedom. Same as you, I suppose. As for Colby, well, something's different in him already. Without you here to lean on, he's growing minute by minute and you'd find his newfound confidence as attractive as I do.*

*Oh, Silas. How can I ignore it any longer? I suppose I'm writing to tell you how sorry I am to have stolen him from you. Please, come home. If you return, I'll leave him to you fair and square. You crave him as much as I do, that much is apparent. And he showed you more hunger than I've ever been able to coax from behind his restraint.*

*I suppose that's truth of why I ran. When I saw you...in the barn. It's important to me that you understand.*

*The sight terrified me. It's been the three of us for so long. How can I live alone? Separated? Hell, we are now anyway. It's not right, Silas.*

*The way you touched him, the way you both grappled to get closer, it knocked the wind from me. Not because your raw desire horrified me, quite the opposite, but because the passion on your faces convinced me I'd lost you both.*

*Neither of you has coveted me with such ferocity.*

"The fuck we haven't!" Silas roared to the empty ranch house. "How could you think that, Lucy?"

Even as he asked, he rewound time and imagined viewing the past through her lens. He'd done his best to preserve her innocence—to protect her from the savage needs raging inside him. Time after time he'd fucked up by trying to shelter her and Colby when he should have admitted they were tough enough to take what he had to give.

He refused to insult them any longer.

He'd finish reading this letter. Then all the others, every last one. Ten years of history through the eyes of the woman he loved. Had always loved.

Tonight he'd come clean. He'd put his soul on display and stand naked before them, all faults exposed, allowing them to decide his future.

Their future.

Until then, he'd hope for a miracle. He'd need one to ensure it wasn't too late.

# Chapter Six

Victoria called out as she climbed the stairs, giving Silas a heads up before she intruded on his thoughts. It wasn't as though Lucy, Colby, or both, entertained him. He should be so lucky. After the hours he'd spent reading, he doubted they planned to return this century.

He winced as he recalled one particular note he wouldn't forget anytime soon. Lucy had vented her anger, calling him every name in the book and some colorful variations he gave her kudos for inventing. The scathing rebuke followed a spur of the moment visit she'd made to the fishing hole he and Colby had often frequented. Truthfully, they'd done more goofing off than actual fishing. The secluded spot had sheltered them from prying eyes and ears when—in the early days—the burden of Colby's past had threatened to smother the teenager with darkness.

Lucy had described the anguish she'd witnessed on her fiancé's face when she'd happened upon him. She'd hidden in the brush, horrified, when the man she loved dropped to his knees and sobbed, begging forgiveness for moving on without Silas as part of their relationship. Her justified outrage had crackled throughout the missive, which included several scratch-outs deep enough to tear her pretty, floral stationary.

The worst of the damage to the note centered around her accusation that he'd tarnished the joy she felt every time she glanced at the token of Colby's fidelity and devotion. The engagement ring she'd prized studying in the sunlight seemed a little dirty after that day.

For that alone Silas owed her more apologies than he could utter in a lifetime.

"Silas!" His mother spoke as she rounded the corner. "Lucy and Colby are running late. Mr. Thead had to have an extra infusion and one of the fences in the west pasture needed mending. But your brothers would like to talk to you."

When she took in the pile of paper covering the mattress, she stutter-stepped but recovered quickly. She smiled, nodding in his direction.

"Are Seth, Sam and Sawyer online?" He checked the clock. With the wide variety in their time zones, it was rare they all were available to gather together for a quick conversation. They managed it when they could.

"I guess. Seth called. He said something about a web whatsit."

Silas barked a laugh. He'd done more of that in the last twenty-four hours than the past several years. "If you hand me my laptop, I'll show you."

Vicky passed him the computer then kissed his cheek while he got things up and running. "You're looking better already."

"Thanks. For everything." He smiled at his mother, unsure of what more to say. She understood anyway.

"Would you mind cracking the window?" He craved the fresh air he'd sampled yesterday and the sounds of the country at night. The cool breeze would help mitigate the raging inferno in his belly, ignited by the hundreds of letters he'd read today.

"Have you forgotten how chilly it is at night?"

"Are you kidding? Hell, most of the drafty places I stayed in were colder in the middle of a summer day."

She winced but didn't argue. Instead, she shrugged and did as he asked.

Silas logged on to the web conferencing service Sam used for business. In the late evening, Eastern Time, no one in the New York office minded them hopping on the line. Hard to believe his little brother had become a powerful stock analyst on Wall Street. Silas had cracked up when he heard they called him The Cowboy.

A series of three dings proved Seth, Sam and Sawyer waited for him to join. He selected their names from the list onscreen then entered the conference.

"You should have seen them. Smoking hot quadruplets, Sam." Silas's brother out west bragged to his twin. "Two for you, two for me."

"Sawyer Compton, what kind of trouble are you digging up now?" Vicky laughed at the horror on her youngest son's face.

"Dude, a little warning would have been nice before you tossed Mom on the line." To see the Coastie blush made Silas's day.

Four pictures divided his screen. He'd placed the images of his brothers as they were situated around the country. His window on top. Sawyer—in San Francisco—on the left, Sam—in New York—on the right and Seth—in Texas—at the bottom.

"Hello, my sons." Vicky tried a finger wave, giggling at the reflection of herself on the screen.

"Hi, Mom." Funny how the appearance of one small woman could change them all in an instant.

"All right, I can tell I'm crashing this party. Just had to see my boys a second. Have fun and call me soon. I love you."

A chorus of "Love you too" echoed through the crappy, built-in speakers.

As soon as the door shut, Silas announced. "Okay, she's out."

"How much of that did she hear?" Sawyer adjusted his uniform. He must be on a dinner break.

"Obviously I missed a good story. Nothing but the last few words came across. You're clear."

"Holy shit, I almost had a heart attack."

"Her and JD aren't exactly prudes." Seth—kicked back in jeans and no shirt with a beer in hand after a long hard day—supplied some dirt. "I heard from Jim Spade they tore it up in the day. Plus, remember the time Sam walked in on them in the kitchen?"

"Gross. I could have gone my whole life without thinking about that again, fuckwad." Sam rolled the sleeves on his expensive shirt to his elbows. Knowing him, he'd planned to head out soon to wine and dine some sophisticate at a restaurant so exclusive, Silas could only imagine what it'd be like.

He'd probably hate it.

"Moving on…" Seth grinned. "How the hell are you, bro? Surly as ever, I guess. The mountain man beard is a nice touch."

"Better today than yesterday." Silas noted the real concern beneath the teasing. As the oldest brother, he'd always been the one to look after them, not the other way around. "Can't wait to climb out of this bed. Maybe take Rainey for a ride."

"Why not stay there? Give Lucy a go, instead. Hell of a lot more fun than a middle-aged horse." Sam laughed at his crass joke. No one else did. "Oh, fuck. Too soon?"

"Moron." Seth shook his head.

Silas growled. "Don't talk about her like that.

She's married."

Not that he hadn't thought the same thing himself a time or two today.

"To a man who's as hot for you as she is." Sawyer didn't zip his big mouth despite the glare from Seth. "How long are we gonna pretend we don't notice them begging for scraps of information from us? How many times are we gonna let Silas fuck things up? One of these days it'll be too late. If I had that kind of love in my life, I sure as shit wouldn't waste it."

"It doesn't freak you guys out? The whole Colby thing?" Silas had struggled with sharing his bisexuality with his brothers for years. Could it be that easy?

"I don't care to hear the play by play, but who you fuck is your business." Seth acted as the spokesperson. The twins nodded agreement. "If I can stand to listen to Sawyer go on about his whips and chains, I think I can handle you getting moony over a guy we all respect."

"I think it's kind of hot." Sawyer shrugged. They all knew of his penchant for BDSM. Power games appealed to their youngest brother. "Not my thing exactly, but I can see how having another guy submit would be a turn on. Don't act like you've never shared a woman with another dude, Sam. You have. And you liked it."

"Sawyer—"

"No, the kid's right." Silas shrugged when all three of his brothers stared, speechless. "I've done a lot of thinking lately. More today."

He grabbed a handful of crumpled envelopes and let them rain around him. "I won't hide who I am anymore."

"You read her letters." Sam's eyes went as big as silver dollars.

"Holy shit." Seth dropped his feet off his desk,

leaning closer to his monitor for to better inspect the background. "They're everywhere."

"What was in them?" Sawyer had always been curious. "I can't tell you how many Christmases, Thanksgivings and nights I spent on leave that I'd watch little Lucy huddled with a pad and a pen, writing like mad. She never gave me a peek, though. What did she write you?"

"Everything." Silas grimaced when his voice cracked a bit. "It's the best gift I could have imagined. A time machine. Every bit of the ten years I missed, it's all here. There were even some pictures."

He held up a few snapshots for his brothers to check out.

"Ohhh, did she include good bits too?" Sam wiggled his brows. "Nasty stuff?"

Silas chose not to inform his brothers of the detailed account of the night Colby had taken Lucy's virginity. Or the night he'd proposed. Silas figured if he kept reading straight through to tomorrow he might find their wedding night in the heartfelt notes she'd kept as religiously as a diary.

"Damn! She *did* write about that stuff. Look at his face."

Before Silas could make them fuck off, a distraction deflected the heat from his revelation.

A sassy voice called out from somewhere, "Tell your brothers it's not nice to kiss and tell. Well, I suppose this Lucy did, but sharing a note with a lover is different than tossing those fantasies to a pack of rabid, ungrateful, fickle cowboys."

"Who the hell was that?" Sawyer jumped at the rebuke.

"Only the cowgirl your fucking asshole brother is keeping prisoner in this godforsaken shack. Will someone please call 911?"

Seth grinned into the camera before tossing over his shoulder, "Don't make me gag you, darlin'."

"Holy shit." Sam leaned closer to the camera. "What is that in the background? Do I see pretty ankles tied to the end of your bed, Seth?"

"I'm Jody Kirkland! My dad is your brother's boss. He'll probably also be the man to murder this piece of shit, arrogant, limp dick when he finds out what he's up to."

"I'll give you arrogant, but I'm guessing Seth's anything but a limp dick right now, honey." Sam braved his brother's wrath.

Silas agreed. A woman that spirited would be worth a black eye or two.

"Argh! You're all alike. I can't believe there are really *four* of you. Thank God you spread yourselves out. No state should have to house that many Compass brothers. Especially if you're all as dense as Seth."

"I like this girl." Sawyer grinned in response.

"So, you're calling the police?" The legs thrashed at the corner of the mattress.

"I don't think my mom would appreciate Seth missing out on the next ten Christmases because he's in jail." Sawyer winked at his brothers. "Sorry, honey. I bet he could help you make the most of the situation."

"You're all bastards. Every one of you asshats!"

"Jody. Give me two minutes. Then we'll talk, okay?" Seth's exasperated groan spoke volumes. Silas didn't try to hide his enjoyment of his brother's frustration. At least he wasn't the only one who did stupid shit when his guts were in a knot. "Si, I swear I thought I'd crapped my pants when they told me you'd almost blown up. So I'm going to say this flat out. I know you're still on the mend but ignoring what Lucy and Colby are offering would be ridiculous."

"Says the man talking to his brothers instead of

playing with the sexy woman tied to his bed, about to escape."

Silas enjoyed the hell out of the surprise on his brother's face. Sam and Sawyer showed their appreciation with whistles and catcalls.

"What!" Seth spun in his chair. When he spotted Jody—naked, in the camera's line of sight as she undid the last of the knots—he lost it. He snagged a blanket off the foot of his bed then wrapped it around her. "What the hell do you think you're doing?"

"Leaving, moron!" She thrashed in Seth's embrace until his brother hefted her over his shoulder, bundled in the blanket.

"Okay, as fun as this is, I have to be on deck in five minutes." Sawyer grimaced. "Someone better fill me in later."

"No, there will be no filling in!" Seth marched to the camera, blocking it with his palm. "I have to go, Si. We'll talk more. Soon."

His connection terminated with a generic beep, leaving Sam and Silas alone on the line. They looked at each other and laughed.

"Almost time for me to hit the city, bro." Sam stretched, taking his suit coat from a hanger behind him.

"Hot date?"

"Sort of. Been spending some time with a girl I work with." His grimace promised it could spell disaster. "I think she's worth the risk."

"Trust your gut, Sam. I should have done the same a long time ago."

His brother nodded. "I'm glad you're home. Safe."

"When are you coming to visit?" Sam made it out to Compass Ranch almost as infrequently as he had. "It's not the same without you three around to piss me off."

"Too hard to fit in a trip. I'm in the running for VP, Si." The corners of his brother's mouth kicked up. "I'd be the youngest in the history of the company."

"We all have our dreams, Sam." Silas couldn't begrudge his brother a shot at his. "Good luck."

"You, too." Sam smiled. "I think you're going to need it."

Colby slid from his horse, exhausted and sweaty. Dozens of snags had mutated his light day into a saga of never-ending hassles. From cowboys fist-fighting over a woman, to a handful of sick steers, to a busted fence, the ranch had conspired against him quitting early. He couldn't wait to find out how Silas had spent his time alone.

"I can take care of Couper for you," Jake offered when he caught Colby peering at the house. "I don't mind, foreman."

"Thank you." He slapped the man on the shoulder. "I'll cover you next time, deal?"

"Deal."

Colby glanced at the light shining from the upstairs window. Was Lucy in there, comforting their man, already? A twinge of unease ran through him. What if Silas only chose her? What if Colby fooled around with Silas and it didn't make him as hot as he thought?

Okay, really, now he was being ludicrous.

Colby had never sought the company of another man, but he and Lucy had talked frankly about how much the idea fired him up. Big time. They'd even played with some toys. It hadn't seemed the same, so they'd stashed the gadgets in their nightstand drawer.

Every now and then, when Lucy treated him to one of her spectacular blow jobs, she'd ream his ass with one of the moderate dildos. The combination spurred him to shoot so hard he feared he'd hurt, or worse, scare her. He never did. She would peek up at him with an evil grin then swallow the huge load he'd pumped down her throat.

Speak of the devil. The high-beams of his wife's Jeep surprised him as they flooded the yard. He strode to greet her with one last tip of his hat to the ranch hands. "Looks like you had the same kinda day I did, baby."

He handed Lucy down from the vehicle, taking her into his arms despite the fact that he stunk to high heaven. She didn't seem to mind.

"If you mean a royally sucky one, then yep." She rested her head on his chest, as though she absorbed strength from his embrace.

Colby adored providing for her.

He wrapped his hand around her elbow then escorted her into the house. As they passed through the kitchen, Vicky removed plates from the warming drawer and put them on a tray along with several beers. He studied the contents as he balanced it on one arm. "Three dinners? Silas hasn't eaten yet?"

"Stubborn boy insisted he'd wait for you two." Vicky smiled then kissed Colby and Lucy on the cheek. "JD and I are heading into town for a movie if you don't need us. Rick and Janice Lowell have been asking us to stop by for ages to check out their new guesthouse, too. You know how it is when JD and Rick start tossing back and shooting the shit. If they talk us into staying, we might not see you kids until tomorrow."

Colby hugged her extra tight. He was nobody's fool anymore than he was still a kid. "Thank you, Vicky."

"Welcome." Silas's mother squeezed Lucy's

hand. As he and his wife climbed the hardwood stairs together, they heard Vicky calling, "JD Compton, get your ass in gear or we'll be late."

The threat worked. JD insisted on being on time for things. Before he and Lucy paused outside Silas's door, the engine to JD's truck turned over. Colby exchanged a long look with his wife. She smiled and nodded. They were ready to discover the possibilities together.

They held hands as Lucy knocked softly on the paneled door. "Silas?"

"Come in."

Lucy opened the door since Colby carried the tray. She stopped short in front of him, nearly causing him to smash their dinners between them. When he'd managed to control the wobble and rebalance his cargo, he noticed what had captured his wife's attention.

"You read them." A grin spread across Colby's face.

"Yeah." Silas patted the bed next to him. "Come here, sweetheart."

Lucy glanced over her shoulder for Colby's nod before sprinting across the small space and hopping onto the mattress. She laughed and dove through the crumpled envelopes as though they were a pile of fall leaves.

Silas tugged her closer, limiting her movement.

"Oh, shit, sorry. Did I jostle you?"

"I'm not delicate, Lu." Silas sat up straighter and hugged her. He kissed her cheek with infinite tenderness that threatened to close Colby's windpipe. How long had he waited to witness something like this?

"You look better today." His wife fit so well in his best friend's hold. She leaned back a little to study Silas.

"Feel better." He smiled into her eyes. "All

because of you. These letters. Colby's understanding. All of it. I can't figure out where to start."

"How about with dinner? You need to eat, and so does Colby."

"I think I better hit the shower first or I'll ruin the chair." He did a quick sniff check and nearly passed out. "Definitely a shower."

"Want me to run your jeans through the wash?" Lucy offered.

"That bad, huh?" Colby examined his soiled clothes. "Yeah, I guess we better."

"There should be a pair of gym shorts in my duffle." Silas jerked his chin toward the bag on the floor. Then his eyes turned dark, hungry. "Or you could go without."

A tiny moan escaped Lucy, breaking the moment and making them all laugh.

"How 'bout you two concentrate on eating dinner and we'll see where things go from there?" Colby grinned when two gazes followed his progress around the room. He couldn't help but rile them further.

He toed off his boots then sidled into the bathroom to flip on the shower. When he'd adjusted the water, he shouted over his shoulder. "I'll leave the door open so I can hear in case you need anything."

Dual stares burned into his back as he shrugged his cotton button-down shirt from his shoulders. He dropped the garment into the hamper then ripped open his fly. Thank God. The pressure had been strangling his hard cock all day.

He peeled off his socks then tucked his fingers into his waistband and nudged his jeans until they dropped to his ankles. He stepped out of the denim then bent to deposit the rest of his dirty clothes in the laundry.

"Jesus!"

A girly giggle followed Silas's rough exclamation. "Hungry, Silas?"

"Starved."

"Go ahead and eat, then Lucy and I can swap." Colby called out. He couldn't resist one peek over his shoulder as he stepped into the shower. The naked lust on Silas's face matched the longing on his wife's. His cock jumped at their attention.

He slathered himself with suds, taking a world-record breaking shower. He made sure to wash all the important bits but forced himself to stop soaping his shaft when it would have been easy to lose control. So easy.

Colby rotated, allowing the water to sluice down his back and run between his ass cheeks. He canted forward, taking the spray against his sensitive hole, imagining what it would be like if it were someone's fingers—or tongue, or cock—caressing him instead.

Precome dripped from his crown onto the shower floor where it swirled in the eddy before disappearing down the drain. His plan almost backfired when he cupped his balls with one palm, fitting the other over the head of his cock.

"You're taking an awfully long time in there, foreman," Silas shouted from the other room. "Your dinner is getting cold."

The strangled sound that emerged when he tried to yell a retort betrayed him. Lucy and Silas laughed between the clinking of forks and knives on their plates. He shut the water off with a snap then toweled dry. He didn't trust himself to tempt them more than he already had.

Not yet.

When Colby wrapped the terrycloth around his waist, he realized hiding his erection would be impossible. He debated for all of ten seconds before deciding, what the fuck? No time like the present. He strode from the room, completely naked and obviously aroused.

"Is that our dessert?" Lucy collected Silas's empty plate, stacking it on her own, before kissing his cheek and heading toward the bathroom.

"Could be." Colby smiled, a little unsure of how to proceed.

"Why don't you tuck under the covers and eat your dinner while Lucy cleans up?"

The chill in the room couldn't account for the shiver that shook him at Silas's suggestion. He did as directed, twisting the top off a beer from the tray then digging in to his food. Sitting side by side with Silas, their shoulders leaning against the headboard, seemed surreal. He focused on the home cooking filling his growling stomach.

"I'd do just about anything for a big swig of that." Si reached toward the bottle. "Do you mind?"

"Should you drink when you're taking pain killers?"

The other man hesitated with his hand wrapped around the dewy brown glass.

"I haven't used any today. I won't be doing that again." Silas shook his head. "Between you and me, I'm done with *all* the hard stuff. Booze included. Kick my ass if you see me slipping, but I need a sip or two to make it through the next hour."

"I understand." Colby put his hand over Silas's on the beer, squeezing. He couldn't imagine how hard it had been for the other man so far from home. Lost in thought, he left his fingers there a little too long and things became awkward. He laughed, hating how nervous he sounded. "This is kind of weird after all this time."

"It is." Silas rounded on him, the newfound

honesty he'd sworn to live by evident in his stormy eyes. "But we'll work it out. It'll become normal. Natural."

"You've done this before?" Colby hated the jealous prickle that climbed the nape of his neck. Hell, he'd spent the last ten years making love to Lucy every chance he found. Silas had to have had someone to turn to for companionship, for relief.

"With another guy?" Silas scrubbed his hand over his face then took a gulp of beer. He placed the bottle on the far side of Colby's tray, away from himself. "Yeah. Lots of times. Would you hand me my shaving kit from my bag when you're done?"

Colby shoveled the last bite of mashed potatoes into his mouth to keep from cursing or having to answer at all. He couldn't risk blurting the wrong thing. His appetite diminished, he swung from the bed to retrieve Si's razor and the warm bowl of water sitting nearby.

As Silas removed layer after layer of whiskers, exposing his bare skin to the elements for the first time in a long time, Colby stewed. He picked at the blankets, trying not to stare at the familiar visage Silas revealed. Without facial hair, he reminded Colby of the young man he'd known. The friend he'd lost. The guy who'd left them to fuck a swath across the Arctic.

Was he angry? Jealous? Envious?

Lucy saved the day when she reappeared. Nothing obscured her beauty.

"Son of a bitch." Silas gawked so hard at the seductive curve of her pert breasts and the dip of her trim waist, Colby expected drool to gather at the corners of his mouth. The other man groaned when his wife did a sultry turn in the middle of the floor, shaking her ass and running her fingers down to her bare mound.

"I guess we both did a little trimming." She

giggled. "You look handsome, Si."

"You're even sexier than I imagined, Lu. And I fantasized about it a lot."

"You did?" She nibbled her lip.

"Yeah, almost constantly." Si held out his hand and she approached to accept it. "I read those letters today, Lucy. I couldn't believe, all this time, you were scared I didn't find you attractive."

"What?" Colby's jaw dropped. "Baby, how could you think that? He used to lose it every time you came near."

"I know, right?" Silas's mouth twisted. His smile held a huge dose of cynicism and disgust. "I guess I did a great job of hiding my lust from her when she was too young. If she hadn't been so damn innocent she would have seen right though me. Like you did."

"All I could think about was how you two looked together." She probably didn't realize her hand had wandered to cup her breast as she recalled the fateful evening. "You were so wild, so hungry, so perfect."

"Would you like a repeat performance, now that we're all clean and fed?" Colby noticed Silas's cock tenting the sheet as much as his own did.

Lucy blinked, as though trying to concentrate on practical matters. "I didn't have time to do more than eat while you were in the shower. I didn't give him his medicine or help him clean up. Are you okay, Si? Do you need pills? Do you feel clean?"

"No."

"I can give you a sponge bath."

Both men groaned.

# Chapter Seven

"While that's tempting, it isn't what I meant." Silas hung his head, something Colby didn't remember the proud man ever having done before.

His wife carried a porcelain basin to the sink in the bathroom and filled it with hot, soapy water. Colby swung his frame from the bed and toted the heavy load for her.

Damn woman never asked for help.

She whipped the quilt and sheet from the bed, exposing Silas to their roving stares. Despite the dozens of marks dotting his skin and the immobilizing brace keeping his femur in line, his physique still stole Colby's breath. "Holy shit."

"What he said." Lucy ogled Silas's thick cock, licking her lips, but their friend didn't seem to understand at first.

"They put a metal rod in my thigh. If someone leaves my crutches where I can reach them I might try them out tomorrow."

"Not by yourself. You'll wait until Colby can spot you." Lucy still didn't avert her gaze. "Roll over, Si."

"If I do, you won't be able to stare at my cock anymore."

She had the decency to blush. "It's more important to wash you clean."

"It'll take a hell of a lot more than a sponge bath to do that, sweetheart." Silas accepted Colby's hand as he scooted lower on the mattress then sprawled onto his front. He lifted his hips to arrange his enormous package.

The motion wiggled his ass, making Colby groan.

"Tell us about it, Si." Lucy dunked the sponge in the warm, soapy water then drew it over Silas's shoulders. She spent extra time swirling the moist material across the tattoo of Compass Ranch. "We're here. We're listening."

"I'm afraid I'll scare you both off."

"We'd never judge you." Colby watched, mesmerized, as his wife continued to soothe the man they both cherished. After she'd finished washing and drying a portion of Silas's skin, Colby couldn't help himself from joining in. He massaged the spaces between Si's injuries, gratified when tension left bunched muscles where he rubbed.

"The more I read today, the more I realized how *wholesome* you both are." He sighed deep enough for the persistent rattle in his lungs to echo in the room. "Colby, you messed around with a couple girls in high school, but once you hooked up with Lucy, she was all for you."

"And I've only ever been with Colby." Dunk, swish, dry. This time across Silas's lower back and the upper swells of his ass.

"Damn, sweetheart. That's so hot to me." Silas's hands started to fist on the sheets until Colby flattened them once more. "I'm not proud of it, but I spent a lot of nights trying anything to warm up inside. I fucked a ton of women. And men. I was always careful, always used protection, still…"

"You think we'd reject you because you've had a lot of partners?" Lucy tilted her head as she moved on to Si's powerful thighs, careful not to press too hard around the area of his fracture.

"I think you should. Not only because of how many there were but also because I did it without an ounce of caring."

"Not even for Red?" Lucy concentrated on washing Silas's feet.

A strangled groan burst from him when Colby followed in her wake, massaging Silas's heels, pressing into the fleshy part of the soles with his thumbs.

"How do you know about Red?" Silas's question crackled with all the emotion he claimed not to have felt.

"I spoke to him on the phone a few months ago. I, sort of, called you every once in a while. Sorry for all the hang-ups." Lucy nudged Silas's hip. "Over."

Colby helped him roll onto his back. Silas's hard cock flopped onto his belly with a thud. "Okay, Red was different. Maybe, if I hadn't already loved you both, I could have been happy with him. I should have made him leave."

"You aren't responsible for what happened, Silas." Lucy paused her nurturing to kiss his scrunched eyelids.

"Maybe."

Colby rubbed Si's scalp, helping him relax again. Without pain pills, sitting in bed all day had to rip up such an active guy. "Look at me, Silas."

When the man complied, Colby leaned close. "We accept you despite your faults. If abandoning us for ten long years didn't tear us apart, then you sleeping around to fill the void won't do it either. If I hadn't had Lucy all this time, I have no idea what I would have done. At least you used protection."

"And I got tested. Every month." He winced. "There was a lot of shit circulating in those bunkhouses. I made sure I'm clean. I'd never put you at risk like that. Either of you. I just... needed to share. In case you're still interested in something more."

Colby couldn't stop himself from eliminating the gap between them. He fused his lips to Silas's, half-braced for rejection even now. He shouldn't have worried.

Si buried his fingers in Colby's damp hair and tugged him closer, devouring his mouth. Lost in the moment, he didn't realize the pressure on his cock was caused by more than the throbbing he'd experienced for two days straight. When Silas moaned into his parted lips, Colby cut his eyes toward his wife.

Lucy held a cock in each hand, pumping in time to the thrust of her men's tongues between each other's lips. Fuck, that was hot. He broke the kiss, needing a breath of air.

Silas coughed beneath him.

"Are you okay?"

"Fuck, yes." Si's head dropped against his pillows when Lucy finished scrubbing his chest and abdomen.

She trailed the sponge and her wet fingers along the ridge of muscle leading from Silas's hip to his groin. "This has to be the sexiest muscle on earth."

"Hey, I have that one too." Colby grinned.

"Maybe you should let me compare them side by side."

"I think your wife is up to something wicked," Silas warned.

"I learned a long time ago it's best not to put up a fight when her eyes have that glint to them." Colby beamed at her as he lay beside his best friend. The heated length of their fit bodies tucked together.

"You're so warm." Silas panted. "Finally, warm."

"Spread your legs. Both of you."

They obeyed without question. Without hesitance. Colby draped his left leg over Silas's right, the uninjured, thigh. Lucy knelt with one knee on either side of their stacked legs. The position spread her pussy, which pressed against Colby.

"Oh, shit." He groaned. "You should feel how wet she is. Scorching my thigh."

"Lucky bastard." Silas grinned. "But I can smell her arousal. Sweet. I bet she's delicious."

"She is." He smiled up at his wife, recalling the feast he'd made of her two nights before.

"Sweet and dirty too." Lucy laughed. "We're about to play a game. I'm going to suck you both. Whoever holds out longer gets to fuck me. Feel free to sabotage each other however you like."

Silas turned to Colby and growled, "You're going down."

"No, I am." Lucy chuckled around Silas's shaft as she pumped Colby with her petite hand. Her soft skin always had him harder than a rock in seconds.

"Oh, damn." Si shuddered. "You don't play around. She took me balls deep on the first pass. Not many women can do that."

"I've been training her for you." Colby grinned. "You're welcome."

"I owe you. Big time."

"Then show me what *you've* learned. Teach me how to be with another man. What do you like, Si?"

The man beside him hesitated. "Uh…"

Lucy pulled her mouth off Silas's cock with a slurp. Her familiar touch engulfed Colby's hard-on, pushing him dangerously close to the edge within seconds. Lying with the two of them ranked high on his list of fantasies.

Less distracted, Silas focused. "You don't understand. I never made love to another man. I've fucked them, sure. Nothing more. I, uh, I've never kissed a guy before. Or any women while I was away for that matter."

"Give me more then." It thrilled Colby that Silas had saved something for them alone. He tipped toward the other man, sucking on the tongue plundering his mouth with rough thrusts. Thicker, stronger than Lucy, the differences excited him. Silas's unique taste thrilled him.

His balls gathered, drawing close to his body.

Lucy switched back to sucking Si's cock, her hand teasing Colby's hard-on with expert handling that kept him from losing it while maintaining his pleasure.

"Yes, baby." He encouraged her to take Silas deeper, faster. He needed the man abandon himself to the desire they inspired. "Suck him harder."

"Yes! No!" Silas's hips flexed, fucking his cock farther into Lucy's eager mouth.

Colby added to Si's rapture when Silas guided Colby's hands to the hard nipples decorating Silas's action-figure chest. Colby flicked his fingers over the sensitive nubs. Silas nipped Colby's lip, encouraging a more aggressive touch, so he pinched the dense, gathered skin and accepted the resulting groan and curse as reward.

Lucy lifted off Silas's cock with a pop. "I think he's close, Colby. I can taste him and the head of his cock is more defined against my tongue. Help me make him explode. I want to drink his come."

His wife's dirty talk had unintended consequences. Aching desire bubbled in Colby's balls. The base of his cock tingled . He was done for.

"Ungh." The first contraction of Colby's orgasm felt like it harvested seed from the tips of his toes. He moaned several more times in rapid succession.

"Oops." He heard Lucy's hybrid laugh and moan when jets of white fluid sprayed over her hand and his abdomen.

"Oh, shit." Silas knocked her fingers aside and milked the rest of Colby's ecstasy from him. All the while they kissed, long and deep, until Silas wandered along Colby's jaw, down his neck, to stare at the evidence of his lust pooling in the dips between his honed muscles.

Colby had never been as proud of his body or his orgasm as he was now. His two lovers radiated appreciation from every pore. Lucy leaned closer and lapped at the opalescent fluid dotting his still-heaving torso.

"Come here." Silas's command would have been impossible for either of them to resist. Lucy turned, her lips glistening in the light from the table lamp. Silas reached for Colby's wife, guiding her up until he could capture her mouth and sample the product of his efforts. "Fuck, yes."

Colby decided to go for broke. He swiped his forefinger through the thickest of the gel then raised it to his partners. Silas ingested his come, leaving Lucy searching for relief.

"She needs your cock, Silas."

"Find me a condom."

"No." Lucy rebelled. She carefully positioned herself above Silas's hips. "I want you bare. You said you're careful. Tested. Clean."

Silas nodded. "But I'm still not your husband. What if you get pregnant?"

She cut her eyes to Colby, who agreed with her. "You're planning on sticking around to raise our kids, right?"

"What?" Silas's purple hard-on flagged a little.

"You'd want that? What would people say?"

"I only give a fuck what you and my wife think." Colby reached between the two people he loved most and took hold of Silas's cock. He positioned the hefty tool between his wife's legs. "Lower yourself onto him, Lu."

She dropped a bit, until the blunt head spread her delicate lips. Silas's girth would stretch her more than his. He hoped it wouldn't cause her pain but, even if it did, she'd relish every moment. So why did she hesitate?

"What's wrong, Lucy?"

"I'm afraid I'll injure him." She rotated her hips, teasing. The motion didn't make much progress in fitting Silas inside her.

"You're killing me. Right now." Silas had forgotten his objections. "Don't stop. You could never hurt me. Not like this. Needed this for a lifetime."

Colby rubbed the remaining traces of his orgasm into his six-pack then knelt behind his wife, between Silas's spread knees. He banded his arm around her waist. "I've got you, Lucy. He's not bearing your weight."

Colby whispered in her ear, loving the goose bumps breaking out all over her peaches and cream complexion. "I'll make sure you don't jostle his thigh. Hang onto my arm and you won't brace yourself on his ribs either."

"I trust you." She angled her head to kiss Colby sweet and slow. While their tongues tangled, he lowered her, a fraction of an inch at a time, onto his best friend's cock, lifting when the resistance grew too strong only to snug her deeper on the next pass.

"Oh, yes. Yes. Finally. Dreamed of this forever," she whimpered into his mouth. "He's so big."

"She's so tight. Can't believe it's real this time."

Silas had fisted his hands in the sheets at his side. "I was close already. I'm not going to last long."

The panic on Silas's face caught Colby's attention. "I'll make it good for her. Don't worry. Lie back and enjoy, Si. I want to give you both this."

Colby's cock stirred a little when he raised Lucy then lowered her again, using his wife to fuck their lover. He shifted his grip so he could rock her faster, while the fingers of his other hand danced over her clit.

Her breasts bounced, the bottoms of the soft globes bobbing on his forearm.

Lucy stared at Silas and the other man returned the gaze, never even blinking. "Perfect. Better than I imagined. Oh, God, Lucy."

His wife started making the tiny mewling sound in the back of her throat that meant she'd explode any second. Colby picked her up—forcing the tip of Silas's cock to fuck her entrance a few times —then impaled her on their lover's thick, veined shaft.

Colby wondered just how good that felt.

Penetrated. Stretched. Stroked from the inside. Hopefully, he'd find out soon.

He tipped his head to nip her neck in the exact spot she preferred. She cried out, "Please!"

"You ready?" he asked Silas.

"Can't stop it." The man shouted and drove his pelvis upward, grinding the muscle covered bone there into Lucy's clit. "Coming! Inside her. Yes. Lucy! Colby! I'm coming."

Colby held on tight while his wife spasmed. Her orgasm seemed endless, enduring. Silas roared their names as he pumped Lucy full of his come. After several minutes, their moans faded to sighs and whimpers.

Colby stopped the gentle sways he'd maintained for his wife, lifting her off of Silas's softening cock. A glistening strand of their mingled fluids dribbled from her spread pussy. He placed her on her back beside the nearly comatose man who'd welded himself to their hearts and souls in a shower of sparks.

He had to show them how much sharing this night with them had meant. He wanted to tend to them. To care for them. To provide all they needed. Instead of reaching for the sponge to clean them, he nuzzled between his wife's legs. He blew on her gently, desensitizing her engorged tissues.

Slowly, he licked her tender folds, lapping up the familiar taste of his wife and the exciting new flavor of their lover.

"If you hadn't drained me already, that would make me come again." Silas coughed as his breathing returned to normal. He'd barely confessed when Lucy cried out, bucking in Colby's hold.

Silas angled himself toward her as best he could, cradling her in his strong arms. "Yes, sweetheart. Like that. Just like that. Come for us. Push it out, give him more."

Wetness flooded Colby's mouth. He devoured her with eager swipes of his tongue. When she finally quieted, he kissed her inner thigh then turned his attention to Silas.

When Lucy realized what he intended she cried out, attracting Silas's attention.

"You want to taste me too, Colby?" The other man arched his hips. "Go ahead. Take what you need."

Colby paused, a hairsbreadth from unexplored territory. This was it. He surged forward and licked along the other man's balls then down the length of his shrinking shaft. He wasn't sure what he'd expected but the silky-smooth skin surprised him. It shifted over the core of lingering firmness. He opened his lips then sucked Silas down to the root of his cock.

"Mmm," Silas hummed.

"Oh, yes!" Lucy's delicate frame was wracked by another set of spasms as she watched her husband clean their lover's cock, stealing his first taste direct from the source. Silas held her, soothed her, massaged her clit until all three cried uncle.

"I can't take anymore." His wife laughed, the lighthearted sound cheering his soul. "Not for at least five minutes."

Colby smiled as he repositioned himself beside her, sandwiching her between him and Silas. Despite their long day and the utter relaxation permeating them all, none of them seemed sleepy. After a lengthy silence, Lucy faced Silas. "You've read some of my letters. Now, share Alaska with us. Tell us about where you've been. Was it as beautiful as it looked on all the documentaries I've watched since you left?"

"God, yes." Silas launched into a description of the landscape. The beauty and the terror. Together, they talked long into the night, finally surrendering to exhaustion only when the sun's rays painted the horizon pink and roosters crowed in the distance.

# Chapter Eight

Silas swung into the stable slower than he would have liked. Crutches and barnyards went together like toothpaste and coffee. Sprinkle in a handful of mostly healed, yet still tender, cracked ribs and molasses probably moved faster than he could right now. His muscles burned and he struggled not to hack up a lung. Fucking smoke. A couple hundred feet had never seemed so far.

Still, he hadn't busted his ass on the hike over from the main house. He'd take that.

"Oh, crap!" A cute blonde in a flirty sundress did a double take when she spotted him hobbling along the aisle between the stalls. Someone had converted one of the old tack rooms into an office for her. His savior hustled from the tiny room with a beat-up folding chair before he could object.

"Sit."

"I'm not a dog." Silas grumbled but accepted her surprisingly steady shoulder to lean on while he lowered himself to the rickety seat.

"Worse, you're a man. A mutt would have more sense." She shook her head then jogged to the open doors facing the pasture. He made idle mental notes about the sexy curves she attempted to obscure beneath the floral-print cotton. If the disguise fooled any man he'd be surprised. "JD! Visitor!"

She trotted over to check on him.

"I'm Silas." He held his hand out and she grasped it with a firm shake.

"I figured. Not too many walking wounded around these parts." She flashed a bright-white smile. "Plus, you resemble your dad."

She pushed her thick glasses up her pert nose with the tip of one finger. "I'm Cindi Middleton. I do the books for Compass Ranch."

"And we couldn't set you up someplace a little nicer? Less dusty at least?" Silas swiped a smudge from her cheek, his eyes slitting when the skittish accountant flinched. He'd been back less than a week but his big brother instinct had defrosted already. The young woman tempted him to offer a hug. Something painful lurked in the depths of her light green eyes. She stayed too still, kept her back to the wall. He'd have to remember to find out the scoop from Colby later.

"She won't hear of us building her a real office." JD tucked a pair of leather work gloves in his ass pocket as he strode into the building. "Enjoys being near the horses. Or so she says."

"It's true." She sighed then drew a deep breath. "Something about the smell of the hay and the animals relaxes me. I like the small noises they make and the barn cats keep me company. Have you met the new kittens, JD?"

Cindi beamed as she pointed to a basket in the corner next to her desk. Tiny balls of orange and black fluff tumbled over each other.

"Yeah, I noticed them yesterday. Actually, I was heading over here to bring you this." He held up a mason jar brimming with fresh milk. "Colby told me you haven't been able to find Tweety."

"Not since two days ago." She worried her lip. "I don't think she's coming home. There was a lot of blood."

"Sorry, hon. You loved that fur ball." JD did hug her then. "Sometimes it's better like that. They go out on their own terms, no suffering when there's nothing you could do to help."

Cindi nodded. She accepted the food for her pets, kissed JD on his tough cheek then pivoted before scrubbing her eyes.

"Better hope Lucy doesn't catch you out here, son. Or Colby for that matter."

"Couldn't stay inside a minute more. Too much restless energy."

JD studied Silas with an appraising stare. "Any left after that hike? There's something I need to talk to you about."

When Silas levered himself to his good leg, JD handed his son his crutches then motioned with his chin. "Come say hello to Rainey. I'm guessing it'll be quite a while before you're back in the saddle but at least you can reintroduce yourself."

"Yeah, doctor said it would be at least another two months, maybe as many as four, before I can ditch all this crap." Silas thanked JD silently when the man paused to fiddle with the hardware holding a feed bucket halfway across the barn. He suspected the gesture was all for show. "Then I'll probably need a freaking cane for another six months. Physical therapy for at least a year."

"Could have been worse."

"Don't I know it?" He thought of the email he'd sent to Red's mother earlier, offering the only solace he could. Her son had intended to return. The woman had responded within minutes, thanking him for the gift of knowledge and offering him shelter if ever he needed it.

She seemed to think he'd meant something to her son and that Red would have been pleased his exile had ended—something positive had resulted from the disaster.

Silas grunted as he reached Rainey's stall and leaned on the wall. The gelding snorted then nuzzled him as though they'd come in from the hard ride from his brothers' campsite minutes, not years, ago. The set of the horse's ears displayed his excitement as he lipped Si's outstretched hand, eager to welcome his rider home. He wondered if the horse could tell from his grin how happy it made him to lay hands on the animal again.

"That horse never turned one bit friendlier while you were gone. Grumpy as shit."

"Seems awful nice to me. Always was." Silas cleared his throat and patted Rainey's neck as the animal leaned into his touch.

"He's clear on who owns him. Most creatures are. That bond and respect never change once earned."

"We still talking about Rainey?" Silas would have shuffled his booted feet if he could have.

"Not likely." JD rubbed his side then helped Silas to the chair before sinking onto a bale of hay. "The hell you've been through changes a man, Si. When you brush death like that, up close and personal, you learn quick to quit fucking around. Time is too precious to waste. We're only given so much and then we're gone."

Silas nodded, wondering how his father understood.

"And that's why I'm gonna ask you straight up. What are you planning to do? Stick? Run? What?"

"I can't leave. Never again." Silas sighed and closed his eyes. "I'm afraid to believe but it seems like this could work. Me. Lucy. Colby. It's insane and flawless. Unless…"

"What now?" His father glared at him.

"Do I embarrass you? There won't be any hiding things. Not around here. The ranch is too close-knit for that. I can't keep it under wraps. After all this time, I can't hide anymore."

"I'd rather you didn't try to pretend at all." JD tilted his head. "There's no shame in honest love, Silas. I thought we raised you better than that. Don't you dare dishonor the patience and pure adoration those kids have kept burning for you. That'd be far worse than the shit-storm of gossip that'll fly for a while. Everyone has a kink."

"Oh, yeah?" Silas laughed, pointing discreetly at the young woman dribbling milk from her finger into a kitten's mouth across the barn. "You think Cindi enjoys things rough and nasty? Likes to be spanked or take it from behind maybe?"

"As a matter of fact, I do." JD shrugged. "Not that it's any business of your disrespectful ass, but you're not the first or the last guy to take a roll in the hay in this barn. Hell, these walls have seen a lot of damn action, and I'm not talking about the horses. Sweet Cindi likes to play with the cowboys. Jake and Ray at least have had the pleasure of double-teaming her. I can tell by the way they touch her and, unless I'm off the mark by a long shot, I'd guess there are two or three more who could say the same. Heard whispers she takes 'em all on at the same time. Keeps her from ending up too close to any one of them. Rings true to me, more than cowboy trash talk."

Silas stared at his father, unsure of what disturbed him more—hearing the man speak so frankly about sex or the shattering of the illusion of innocence haloing the timid bookkeeper. "Her? She acted afraid of me. Not the kind of woman to submit to four or five guys, especially not those hulks."

"Not the type. Huh. I imagine a lot of folks would say the same about Lucy. Doesn't make it any less true." JD laid it on the line. "You can't judge what people need until you know them, Silas. Really know them. From what I pieced together, Cindi likes to surrender, once she's satisfied she's in capable hands. If I ever find the bastard who put those shadows in her eyes, I'll kill him myself."

"I'm starting to think our family has grown while I was gone." Silas regretted every minute he'd missed.

"It has. Still, no one could replace you or your brothers. This ranch is your legacy, son." JD looked straight into his eyes. "Are you ready to man up?"

"Sure, with you at the helm and Colby as foreman. I'll work twice as hard as anyone else. I swear I'll do my best to make you proud."

"You always have, Silas." His father sighed. "But you're gonna have to speed things up some."

"What do you mean?"

"I wish I could give you time to settle in. Heal. Take a honeymoon with Colby and Lucy." JD hunched forward, bracing his elbows on his knees. "I can't. *I* need you Silas. Your family needs you. Compass Ranch needs you."

As though a curtain had lifted, Silas noted the slight sheen of sweat on JD's face. Brackets around his father's mouth caused not by age, rather by persistent pain, drew his seeking gaze. Bloodshot eyes and a yellow cast to JD's skin Silas hadn't noticed beneath the tan appeared in the wake of his scrutiny.

"You don't feel well? Head to the house, I'll call Lucy."

"No point, Si." JD shook his head.

Was it this annoying when he went stubborn? Jesus, why had no one kicked his ass by now?

"And I'd prefer to keep this between us if you

don't mind."

Silas's heart hammered when JD's solemn stare locked on him. This was bigger than the flu or some spoiled food at lunch. No!

"I heard you telling Colby about the fire last night."

The two men had sat out on the porch long past midnight while Lucy dozed on the whitewashed swing. He couldn't hoard enough of the fresh air or their company.

"I guess I'm at the point where I realize the alarm bells in *my* system are not caused by some false alarm." As though he'd summoned his own personal demon, JD coughed. When the man yanked his handkerchief from his pocket, Silas noticed tiny flecks of blood spotting the fabric.

Terror spiked through his brain. His invincible father could not be ill. Not like that.

"I'm not ready to call it quits. Or even to start blabbing about what I suspect. But I'm damn glad you're home. Takes a huge load off my shoulders. I've considered calling you back for a couple months now. I only wish, for your sake, that I'd picked up the phone sooner."

"Wait." Silas tried to process everything happening at lightning speed. "Have you been to the doctor? What's wrong?"

"I don't need fancy medicine to discover what I already know." JD sat straighter. "I'm not willing to drag this out in some slow progression that steals every scrap of my pride."

"You can't throw in the towel without trying. You have to make an appointment, get a professional opinion. What if it's something simple? Something easy to fix? Don't be ignorant." Silas raged inside and out. "I may be on crutches, but I will make you do this if I have to knock you unconscious with one and haul your ass there myself."

"I truly did miss you." JD laughed so hard he clasped his side again. "I appreciate the concern. I'm past the point of no return. I'm not gonna waste any of the time I have left on nonsense. Tomorrow morning we'll begin reviewing information, starting with inventory and my five-year plan for operations."

His father checked his watch then made to leave.

"I suggest you wait here. I'm expecting Colby in the next ten minutes. I'll have him help you to the house." JD dropped his hand onto Silas's shoulder. "We can't afford you getting hurt anymore."

His father ambled into the setting sun, his silhouette shrinking as he moved farther away. Silas gasped hard through his open mouth, willing himself to calm. He had to call Seth. Together, maybe they could talk some sense into their crazy old man.

He cursed at the ceiling, his fingers gripping the stall door. Rainey nudged his hand until it rested on the gelding's nose. He stroked the white spot there over and over as he thought of all the possibilities.

Too few of them were positive.

"You've really fixed this place up."

Colby beamed. Silas inspected his handiwork as they leaned against the front bumper of his truck. Colby gave his friend a couple seconds to steady himself before heading inside his and Lucy's house. They'd convinced Victoria and JD it'd be safer for Si to stay at their place, where all the rooms were on one level, rather than risk their stubborn lover tumbling down the stairs if he had trouble sleeping and could no longer suppress the urge to wander.

The trip to the barn and back earlier seemed to have exhausted Silas. Granted, he hadn't undertaken much physical activity since the explosion but, still, it seemed odd for someone as toned as Si. He hadn't suffered from lack of manual labor during his exile— that much was clear.

Colby flexed the well-developed muscles in his back. He couldn't imagine his strength stripped from him. He took the body he'd grown into for granted sometimes. He'd earned every sculpted inch his wife often admired. "I've been finishing projects as I can. Replaced the roof this spring and built the wrap-around porch last fall. Lucy likes to slip on a bathrobe and drink her tea out there in the morning. Not like there's anyone to see."

"I hope you've taken advantage of that perk." Silas grinned at Colby.

"I've had to haul ass to meet the rest of the hands plenty of mornings." He wrapped his arm around Si's waist and helped the man up the stairs, practically carrying him. "Not gonna lie, making love to Lucy on the dewy planks before heading off to early chores is worth sacrificing breakfast, no matter how delicious her omelets are."

Colby ensured Silas had his crutches under him before he knelt to remove Si's boots then kicked off his own. Lucy would kill them if they tracked mud onto the precious maple floors he'd installed for her five years or so ago.

"Jesus. I can imagine." Si still seemed sluggish as they crossed the threshold, but the lascivious thought perked him up. "One taste of her and I'm addicted. She's so hot, so tight. So eager to play."

"Mmm." Colby settled Silas on the wide leather sofa, elevating his braced leg using the ottoman and a few pillows as Lucy had mandated, then shifted the hard-on forming behind his zipper. "I love her so much, it's terrifying."

"Same here." Silas stared straight into Colby's eyes until he couldn't bear it anymore.

He cleared his throat then gestured to the bright plaid curtains and the plant stand overflowing with greenery. "Lu did all the decorating."

"It's nice. Really comfortable." Silas nodded when Colby sank beside him, their hands almost touching where they rested at their sides.

The injured man glanced at the clock above the piano, which no one played, but Lucy refused to sell. A ridiculous prop he tolerated. Anything to make her smile. "When does she call it quits? I don't like the thought of her driving on those deserted roads, alone, after nightfall."

Dusk encroached on the quaint home, sapphire blue sky replacing the orange streaks of the sunset lingering outside the picture window in front of them. "She's usually here by now. It depends on the day and the patients. She carries a cell phone despite the spotty coverage. I've gotten better at beating the worry into submission, but thanks for reminding me."

"Shit. Sorry, Colby." Silas winced. "Believe me, I appreciate how stress can suck the life out of a guy."

Could it be more than physical exertion draining Silas this evening?

"Anything you care to share?" Colby didn't quite know how to be with Silas. Not yet, anyway. So he waded through memories to the times Silas had shouldered some of his burdens. When nightmares of his father's abuse had seeped into his waking hours, Si had noticed and listened. Or distracted him. He'd forged a loyalty strong enough to last a decade, a thousand decades.

Maybe Colby could return the favor.

"Supposed to keep my mouth shut." Silas shook his head.

"Oh, I like secrets," Lucy called from the other room.

How had they not heard her arrive? She must have ridden her mare from the main house. He should have informed her he'd transferred Silas home.

"Tell me?" When she hung her bag on the hook by the door and pranced into the living room, Colby sighed. His wife would fix the lost look haunting Silas's eyes. She hesitated when she spotted the marked difference in their lover.

Lucy understood immediately. This had nothing to do with Si's injuries. Unlike Colby, she saw straight to the heart of the matter in an instant. "What happened?"

She dropped to the floor on her knees between Silas's spread legs, laying her cheek on his good thigh. Her arms banded around his waist, surrounding him with her gentle care. Colby angled himself to face them better, laying one hand on her trembling back and the other on Silas's shoulder.

Si groaned. He buried the fingers of one hand in Lucy's pale hair, kneading her scalp so her silken waves caressed the sensitive span of his palm. His other hand gripped Colby's knee. The ferocity of his hold convinced Colby he clung to sanity by his fingernails.

"We're here for you. Let us help. You're not alone anymore," Lucy whispered but her concern ricocheted around the room with the force of a rifle shot.

"Fuck. And thanks.." Silas dropped his head against the cushion, his eyes closed as though blocking out the world would improve his odds of winning his struggle to maintain composure. "It's different. Hard to adjust. Everything in my life is chaos. I'm used to order, black and white, right and wrong. How can I be in control when everything is gray? My whole life has fucking changed."

"Some things for the better, right?" Lucy peeked at the man she consoled.

Bad day or not, Colby would crush Silas if he hurt his wife.

"Yeah. Shit, yes." Si didn't disappoint. "You're amazing. Both of you. I couldn't do this without you."

"Do what?" Lucy petted his solid abdomen as it flexed with his elevated respiration. Colby fluffed his collar to release some steam despite the dread swirling around them like a cloud.

"Fuck it. JD knows what you mean to me. I don't intend to turn from you ever again. He has to suspect I'd tell you."

"What does your dad have to do with this?" Lucy raised her head, her eyebrows scrunching together as she tried to decipher Silas's ramblings.

The answer became clear as the mountain spring in the west pasture to Colby. All the times he'd caught JD rubbing his side, the persistent cough he played off as allergies, the gruff determination to teach Colby the strategic side of ranching this summer when he'd focused on operations for a decade.

Oh, son of a bitch.

"JD's sick." Colby swung his gaze to Silas's grateful stare. Si hadn't had to break his father's confidence yet he didn't have to tow the line alone. Never again.

"What?" Lucy started to stand but her men kept her in place. "I'll go to him. I can help. I was just at the house. No one said anything."

"They don't know. It's worse than a simple cold or a broken leg, baby." Colby hated the terror in his wife's eyes. She thought of JD as her own father. They all did.

"He's convinced he's dying." Silas stated the

facts in a cold, distant tone.

"No!" Lucy struggled until Colby worried she might hurt Si. He tugged her into his arms, cradling her between his body and Silas's. "It can't be true."

"Nothing's for sure yet." Silas shook off some of his gloom to reassure her. Having a purpose seemed to help the commanding man. "Somehow I have to convince him to see a doctor."

"Between the three of us, we'll wear him down." Lucy's half-hearted attempt fell flat.

"You don't believe that. Unless I missed a shitload more than I thought, my father isn't the kind of man to succumb to badgering."

"Maybe it's time for Seth to come home." Colby spoke softly, serious. "He's learned tons from Kirkland's ranch. If the three of us can prove we have things under control here, it could take some of the pressure off JD. Then I bet he'd consider it."

"You have a point, but Seth has some...*issues* of his own." Silas rubbed his temples. "Let's wait a bit. We might work a miracle. If not, I'll make the call."

"It could be nothing." The rain cloud darkening Lucy's natural glow lifted.

Colby debated correcting her. He couldn't allow them to live with false hope. "I'll be praying, like everyone else, it's something minor. But I can't ignore the signs. He's never slowed down a minute in all the years I've lived here. This summer... I should have put it together. Should have caught this sooner."

"We all should have. I've noticed he seems tired." Lucy whimpered, and Silas stroked her cheek. "I assumed the heat affected him more this year, now that he's a bit older."

"He's such a badass. He makes it easy to forget he and Vicky have so many years between them." Colby nuzzled his wife's neck. "He's close to seventy."

Lucy nodded. "Vicky grumbled about her fiftieth coming up next year."

"Whatever happens, Silas, we'll handle it together." Colby met his friend's gaze over his wife's bowed head. "No more secrets between us. We're one unit, unconventional or not. Aren't we?"

Lucy perked up in time to witness Si's response.

"Fuck, yes." Determination blazed in the man's eyes. "If you'll have me. If it won't interfere with what you two have built. Nothing can tear us apart. I need you. I need what we have together."

"That's right. When the world is crazy outside, we're here." Lucy leaned in Colby's grip to place a calming kiss on their partner's lips. "Never forget. With us, you're in control."

Colby's cock lifted at the implication. Could the time finally be right?

"I've waited a long time for you to claim what's yours." Colby hesitated until Lucy smiled up at him, encouraging. "Take me, Silas? Find peace with me. Please?"

"I can't." Si threatened to splinter his soul.

"Why the hell not?" Lucy jumped to his defense. He didn't think he could beg twice.

"I won't be gentle. Not now." Silas shook his head. "Not like this."

"He didn't ask you to treat him with kid gloves." Lu took Silas's face in her palms, forcing him to meet her determined stare. "He's strong, Si. So strong. He wants all of you. He needs the unbridled passion only you can give him. Show him who owns him. Owns us both. Prove to yourself, you *can* take control."

Quick as a flash flood, and with all the same elemental power, Silas snapped.

He roared, "Bedroom, now."

# Chapter Nine

Lucy wiggled from between the two men sandwiching her on the couch, impatient to obey Silas. With her on one side and Colby on the other, they ducked beneath Si's arms, which bulged with muscle, and helped him the short distance to their bedroom. Her hand swept from his waist over his tight ass, covered with soft cotton sweatshorts, when she released him to stand on his one good leg with Colby for support.

Without waiting for instruction, she knelt before him.

Lucy tucked her fingers into his waistband and stripped the light fabric from his trim hips, down his powerful thighs, careful not to snag them on the immobilizing brace. The ridge of his calves drew her fingers. She explored the furred skin a moment before raising her gaze.

His thick cock dangled, half-hard against his thigh. A flashback to the other night, when he'd packed her full, assaulted her senses. She shivered. An entire lifetime of fantasies hadn't come close to the real thing. She couldn't resist tasting him.

Lucy licked the broad crown capping his cock, sucking him to the depths of her mouth.

"Fuck, yes." He hissed when she flicked her

tongue over the sensitive underside of his shaft. "Get me good and stiff, angel. I'm gonna need one hell of a hard-on to penetrate your husband's virgin ass."

She shivered, moaning around the cock inflating by the second. Her gaze cut to her husband, afraid for a split second of what her abandon might inspire in him. She shouldn't have worried. Lust burned in his gorgeous eyes. And, if she read him right, a little envy.

Colby licked his lips, and she moaned.

When Silas descended onto the bed, she followed him, devouring his shaft while she could still fit the whole thing in her mouth. Wouldn't be much longer until he outgrew her. Already his thick shaft stretched her lips into a tight ring and she couldn't help but graze her teeth over his hard-on.

"Just like that." Silas stroked her cheeks around his embedded cock, smiling into her eyes.

Colby's hand broke her line of sight when he reached between her and Si to peel Si's T-shirt from his ripped torso. Her husband's spectacular muscularity seemed lean compared to Silas's bulk. How much hard living had he done to earn this ideal physique?

"Stand." He tugged her hair hard enough to sting. Her pussy gushed. She released him from her mouth reluctantly.

As much as she savored Colby's gentle loving, she'd be lying if she claimed she never longed for something a little more raw. A teensy bit rougher.

"Undress each other." Silas leaned on one elbow like a sultan observing his harem. He used the other hand to stroke his raging erection.

She didn't react immediately, fascinated with how he touched himself—firm yet gentle in places. Colby must have suffered the same distraction because Silas growled.

"Don't make me repeat myself." He swiped the

bead of precome from his tip with his thumb then massaged it into his engorged flesh as he threatened, "I can still put you over my good knee."

A flash of heat rushed up Lucy's chest, neck and cheeks at the mental image of Silas pinning her to the mattress with one broad hand while the other delivered spank after spank until her wetness ran onto his fingers and Colby cleaned them both.

"I don't think that was an effective deterrent, Si." Colby groaned and took a step closer.

"Then how about this..." The injured man's hips arced off the mattress, thrusting his cock through the ring of his fingers to the base. He looked huge. Long and wide. "If you don't get naked quick, I'll take care of myself."

"No!" Lucy clapped her hand over her mouth, horrified. How could he play her so well?

Colby chuckled as he edged closer, nipping her neck before whispering, "Don't worry, baby. He wants us as bad as we want him. Let's put on a nice show for Si."

She couldn't think clearly enough to do anything more than respond to her instincts, which screamed to touch her men skin on skin. She crumpled Colby's button-down shirt in her fists, one on each side of the center, then yanked. Plastic pinged off the window, the floor and the furniture as the gap revealed his sleeveless undershirt.

"Much better." Silas abandoned his thick shaft, which thudded onto his flexed abs, in favor of cupping his balls. They filled his palm as he rolled them back and forth. "Keep going. Show me every inch of *my* lovers. You are mine. You understand that, right?"

"God, yes." Colby answered in unison with her. They looked at each other and grinned.

She decided to get down to business. The

throbbing in her core wouldn't tolerate her torturing her men much longer. Every instant she tormented them withheld her own pleasure.

Lucy grabbed the hem of her dress and whipped it over her head, leaving her standing before her husband and his ravenous best friend. She wore nothing more than a few scraps of delicate lavender lace.

Colby clutched his chest and Silas's cock twitched on his belly. She smirked over her shoulder as she pivoted then bent at the waist and grabbed her ankles to present her ass. The sight kicked her husband into action. He fell to his knees behind her then stripped the thong from her hips. The tiny line of drenched fabric between her legs brushed her pussy as it separated from her body, making her cry out.

"So beautiful." Silas approved of the goods on display.

His lust spiked her arousal higher. A trickle of moisture ran down her thigh.

"You better not waste that, Colby."

Lucy's knees almost buckled when her husband licked a trail from her knee to her pussy at their lover's instruction. He supported her as he nibbled on the puffy lips bracketing her opening. She arched her hips, hoping he'd spear her with his broad fingers.

"Go ahead, give her what she's asking for." Silas granted her husband permission to stuff her. "Spread her ass. Open her until there's no doubt she's, ready. Then slide in deep."

Her husband followed orders, making her blush as he exposed her to Silas's laser stare. When he penetrated her, all other thoughts fled. She squeezed him, hugging his hand as she welcomed him inside her body.

"Do you ever fuck her ass? Is she into it?"

Lucy wasn't sure what it said about her that she

enjoyed them discussing her as though she weren't right there in the room. She couldn't wait to serve them both, making their fantasies come true as they did the same for her.

"Once or twice." Colby curled his fingers, rubbing a sweet spot inside her. "She came, but I think she prefers when I fill this sweet pussy."

"Someday she'll take us both." Slick slapping sounds reached her ears as Silas jerked himself faster. "I'm gonna fuck that ass while you bury yourself in her pussy. All of us, linked together."

Lucy moaned, a shockwave traveling out from her center to the tips of her fingers and toes.

"She'll come if I'm not careful." Colby kissed her hip, withdrawing a fraction of an inch and easing his knuckle from her clit.

"Already?" Silas groaned. "So responsive. Perfect. Take the edge off, Colby. Grant her release so we can take our time. She can come more than once in a session?"

"Hell, yes." As though Colby couldn't help it, his fingers bottomed out in her rippling sheath. "I think the record stands around a dozen times."

"Sounds like a challenge to me." Si grinned. "I fucking love a competition. As soon as I'm healed, we'll find out who can make her shatter the most."

Lucy couldn't help herself. Her pussy spasmed around her husband's fingers. He spread them, resisting the compression of her climaxing body, even as she clamped down. He extended her pleasure with short jabs through saturated tissue. She didn't realize she'd gone lax until he bundled her in his arms and lowered her to the bed beside Silas.

"Come here, angel," he murmured to her as the world returned to focus. "Did our Colby do a good job? Did he make it sweet for you?"

"Always."

Silas lowered the cup of her bra until her full breast spilled from the garment. He surrounded the heavy mound with his hand, her hard nipple poking his palm, when she rolled onto her side. She jerked in his hold as aftershocks continued to zip along her spine. Unable to speak, she couldn't express how much it meant to share this with them both. He didn't need the promise. The appreciation for their gift must have shone from her eyes.

"This is just the beginning, Lu." Silas slammed his mouth over hers, drawing her tongue between his lips then sucking hard. He overwhelmed her senses with pure greed before breaking away to stare at Colby. "My turn for a taste."

Her husband put one knee on the mattress then extended his fingers. Silas lunged upward, nipping the digits before devouring her juices from them.

"So fucking sweet," he groaned as he collapsed onto the bed. "But we're going to have to work on following directions. Why do either of you still have clothes on?"

Lucy had never seen Colby move so fast. Stitches popped, filling the room with a soft tearing sound when he shed his tank. She didn't realize she'd shifted her hand to her pussy at the sight of all that tan skin until Silas grasped her wrist.

"Did I tell you to play with my pussy?" he rasped.

"Please." She couldn't believe she begged to touch herself. She'd orgasmed not two minutes before for crying out loud.

"No." Silas set her arm at her side, clearly expecting it to stay there. He wedged his hand beneath her, unhooked her bra then removed it from her with one deft movement. "If you need to come again so soon, you'll take pleasure from me this time. If you like, you can stroke my cock while Colby strips for us."

He guided her head to his inclined shoulder as they both lay on their backs, side by side. Their arms crossed as they reached for each other.

"Oh, God." She gasped at the first contact of Si's fingers on her wet slit. Her hand fisted around his steely cock in response. She'd dreamed of this for so long, it almost didn't feel real.

"Mmm." He kissed her forehead before lending his attention to Colby. "Turn around. Wiggle that ass as you strip out of your jeans. When you're naked, I better see a stiff cock, ready to drill your wife. I think she's in need of a more vigorous ride than I can give her with this stupid leg busted up."

"Not a problem." Colby's reply sounded as though it were drawn through a shredder.

Lucy grinned at Silas. No doubt he controlled them. She counted the moments until he healed enough to place her face down, ass up, and deliver on his promises.

Si winked at her then nudged aside her swollen lips. The tip of his finger dipped into her slit and sought her ripe clit.

"Ah!" She angled her head and bit his pec when ecstasy washed through her. Her lingering orgasm rekindled beneath his inflaming touch. "Hurry, Colby."

Her husband swayed from side to side as he worked at the oversized buckle on his belt. She thrust against Silas's hand. Leather hit the floor and the rip of a zipper unknitting reached her ears. Colby hooked his thumbs in the waistband and shimmied from his jeans and boxer briefs simultaneously.

"Gorgeous, isn't he?" Silas asked her.

"Amazing in every way." Tears stung her eyes as she considered how lucky she was to have two men like this in her life.

"Horny as hell too," Colby grumbled but he didn't stop enticing them with the play of his golden form.

Her husband's heavy balls swung between his legs. From the position of his elbows, she assumed one hand played with his cock while the other rubbed his chest. He went bananas when she stroked him there, or licked his peaked nipples, while he fucked her.

"Enough," Silas barked, his erection throbbing in her palm. "Lucy needs your cock inside this slippery cunt. Are you ready to give it to her?"

"I was ready ten minutes ago, Si." Colby spun then, his hard-on jutting from the trimmed brown hair between his legs.

Silas rolled to his side, his injured leg on top. He cradled her shoulders on one arm while the other played with her body. "I can't wait to watch you together. I need to see how it's been."

"I didn't think it could be any better." Lucy cupped his cheek in her hand. "But it is."

Colby nudged the inside of her knees until she spread her legs wide to make room for him. He didn't waste any time in aligning the head of his cock with her pussy. Though he could have thrust into her soaked folds, he glanced to Silas for approval.

"Fuck her slit first. Make your cock dance over her clit."

Lucy wouldn't survive. The glide of her husband's dense, heated hard-on over her delicate nub drove her insane on the best of days. Ultra-erect now, he had to force his cock down with two fingers on the top of the shaft.

"Need a hand?" Silas reached between them to aim Colby's shallow thrusts. The blunt head of her husband's erection tapped her clit, making her eyes roll.

"Yes!"

She wasn't sure who'd shouted it, but she agreed one hundred percent.

"Do you two keep lube around?" Silas grunted when Colby fucked through his fingers harder.

"Nightstand drawer," Lucy cried out when her husband seemed speechless.

"Grab it," Silas ordered Colby, who reached to the side without pausing his pattern of lunges. Her husband handed their lover the mostly-full tube. Knowing what he intended to use it for had her thrashing beneath her man.

"You like the thought of my cock sinking in your husband's ass, don't you?" Silas teased. She responded with something more convincing than a verbal affirmation.

Another orgasm gripped her. Her husband played with her clit, slapping his cock against it as Silas bent to suck her nipple into his mouth. He bit the tip lightly, soothing the sting with his tongue when the prism of light began to fade behind her eyelids.

Colby bent to kiss her, the simple gesture sweet and every bit as enticing as Silas's wicked play. While both men feasted on her, Silas's hand moved between them. He altered the angle of their connection so the next time Colby's hips shuttled forward, his thick erection tunneled inside her humid flesh.

"Ah, God." Her husband rose on straight-locked arms above her, his spine arched. He forged deeper and deeper as though he had no other choice.

Silas patted Colby's flank, encouraging him to work his substantial shaft into her body until they were joined as completely as possible. "There you go, Colby. Right where you want to be."

"Always." Her husband smiled at her before facing Silas. "With you both."

The men leaned toward each other until their

mouths brushed. Their initial hesitance evaporated at the bare connection. Si wrapped his hand around the nape of Colby's neck and welded their lips. They ate at each other with more intensity than she might have found comfortable, but neither let up. Their tongues twined around each other and still her husband fucked into her.

Her body seemed to ride one peak to the next, never dipping into the valley she associated with prior extended loving. Instead of multiple orgasms with a period of rejuvenation, wave after wave of pleasure caught her in their flow. Everywhere she looked—every touch, every sound—was fuel for the fire threatening to consume her.

"Oh, shit." Colby ripped his mouth from Silas. "She's coming. Again. And again."

"Such a good girl, Lucy." Si beamed at her as though she had any control over her body at this point. "You love his cock, don't you?"

"Yes!" she shrieked when another burst of pleasure wracked her.

"Hurry, Silas." Colby fucked her as commanded. Tension drew his shoulders tight. "I can't hold off forever."

"I'm impressed you've lasted this long." Silas laughed. "I gave you less than ten minutes in my mind. This is better. We can all come together. Concentrate, Colby. Don't let us down."

"Low blow, Si." Her husband gritted his teeth and fucked. His head hung between his shoulders.

Silas uncapped the lube and slathered it over his fingers. When he reached behind her husband, = Colby's brilliant blue eyes widened. "Oh God, Lucy. He's playing with my ass, teasing my hole, stretching me open."

Another ripple of delight passed through her cunt,

squeezing her around her husband. She must have screamed because Silas glanced over at her and grinned.

"Keep going."

Colby grunted, whether because Silas sunk his glossy fingers deeper in his ass or because she wrung his cock with her twitching pussy, she couldn't say. She began to float, to observe as though having an out-of-body experience. The three of them fit together so perfectly, anticipating each other's desires. She couldn't imagine anything more beautiful.

"His ass is so hot on my fingers. You tried this with him. Didn't you, Lucy?"

She nodded, her hand gripping Colby's arm.

"I bet my fingers feel different. Don't they, Colby?"

"Thicker. Longer. Damn! So much bigger." Her husband panted, not complaining about the upgrade.

"Wait until you take my cock." Silas bit Colby's shoulder.

"Oh!" The intensity of the pleasure whipping through her increased again. Her clit throbbed where her husband's pelvis brushed it. Nothing had ever felt this good. Nothing.

"Now." Colby shuddered above her when Silas's arm increased its speed. Silas rammed his fingers in her husband's ass harder and harder. "No more waiting. Right now."

Silas laughed, the sound easing her spirit. "Greedy. I like it. You're ready."

"Been ready!"

"Roll onto your side, facing away from me."

Colby lifted her and rotated, his cock never abandoning her sheath. He settled them on the pillows then snugged himself toward Silas. Lucy threaded her hand between Colby's hip and his top arm to rest on

Silas's side. She had to feel him. To maintain their connection.

"Push out. Breathe deep." Silas's worried face appeared over her husband's shoulder as he slicked his cock with excessive lube. She gripped her husband's ass and spread him wide, inviting Silas to take what belonged to him. "This might hurt."

"Nothing could be more painful than not having you," Colby answered for them both. Her heart concurred. She kissed her husband with every ounce of caring she possessed. Every molecule of the longing they'd both suffered through. She lent him her strength and courage. Silas gave her a play by play as he fit the head of his cock to the pucker in the valley of Colby's ass and broached her husband's virgin hole, joining them at last.

"Ah!" Colby went stiff in her arms. His erection wilted a fraction in her pussy. "Christ, you're huge. So fucking bulky."

When Silas would have backed out, she clamped her hand on his hip and drew him tighter to them instead, impaling her husband on their lover's shaft. She rocked her hips, stroking Colby's cock with her pussy even as she coaxed him to kiss her again and ride out the pain.

From the few times they'd played like this, she realized blazing passion would soon eclipse the discomfort.

"That's it. Relax, Colby." Silas moaned. "You're holding me nice and deep now. Almost buried to the balls. You're doing great. Just a little more. So fucking hot. Tight. Sexy."

Lucy shrieked when another mini-orgasm flooded her pussy. Hearing Silas filthy yet reverent whispers destroyed her restraint. Her husband opened himself to another man even as he took her.

"Oh, yes." Colby's smoky tone returned and he began to pound inside her, fucking himself onto Silas as hard as he fucked her. "Her pussy is so hungry, milking me. She loves listening to you, Silas."

"Both of you. Together. Love you both." She stared into her husband's eyes, permitting him to observe the eternal joy he inspired in her.

"I love you too, Lucy." He kissed her long and slow as Silas began to fuck him harder, forcing Colby's cock to glide deep into her. They surrendered, allowing Silas to control the encounter along with their pleasure and their hearts.

"Silas," she cried out as she met his gaze over her husband's shoulder. "God, how I need you."

"We both do," Colby rumbled as Silas plowed into him, his injuries forgotten.

Silas reached over Colby to hold her hand, their fingers entwining as he captured Colby's mouth once more. Then he paused for a split second. He shifted his gaze between them. "I love you too. Both of you. So much."

He slammed his hips into them so hard she was sure he rammed his cock to the hilt in her husband's ass. Once. Twice. Three times. Then he roared the declaration. "Forever."

"He's coming. Lu, he's coming in me." Colby fucked her as he drew the seed from Silas's balls. "Spurt after spurt. So hot. Oh, fuck. Yes!"

The combination of the graphic commentary and her husband's expert loving amplified the extended pleasure swamping her senses. Her entire body gathered, her toes curling. Then she shattered. Colby gripped her tight, fucking her through the storm.

"Give in, Colby." Silas nipped her husband's neck. "Come for us. With us."

Her husband stared into her eyes then

surrendered. "Love. You."

He howled as he emptied his longing, fear and hope into her along with jets of scalding come. She thought it impossible, but her body couldn't resist the lure of his capitulation and joined him in one last bout of rapture.

White light flared behind her eyelids and she sighed, unable to find one single reason to move from the shelter of her men's embrace. Exhausted. Sated. Complete.

Lucy relaxed, slipping into a state of unconscious bliss.

# Chapter Ten

When Lucy awoke, stars shone through the open curtains, which billowed in the breeze Silas enjoyed so much. She lay in their bed, alone. Not acceptable. She glimpsed at the clock, shaking her head. After midnight. The growl of Colby's truck engine had roused her a while ago. She'd been too dazed to investigate.

After blinking a few more times, she grabbed Silas's discarded T-shirt from the floor and ducked into it. The supple gray cotton reached almost to her knees. She climbed from the king-sized bed, surprised she didn't experience more discomfort from their reckless fucking.

Silas could have reinjured himself. If he'd endured any pain he hadn't showed it. The memory of his awe as he conquered Colby's ass would turn her on until the day she died. The bond they'd strengthened overflowed her soul with happiness.

She slipped out the screen door, headed for the shadowy figure in the corner of the porch.

"Is your leg bothering you?" she whispered to the man in the moonlight.

"Nah. That's not it."

"Trouble sleeping?" She crossed to the spot

where Silas leaned against the rail, staring out at the prairie and the mountains in the distance. The purple shadow glowed beneath the full moon.

Lucy wrapped her arms around his waist and snuggled into his bare shoulders after kissing the Compass Ranch brand at the center of his tattoo. The heat pouring off of him made blankets unnecessary.

"Yeah. Colby had to run into town to bail out a couple of the hands. I planned to stay and hold you while you slept but I have a lot on my mind and..."

"What, Si?"

"Damn nightmares." He scrubbed his hand over his face. "I keep playing it over and over. Wondering. Could I have done something different? For Red."

"He chose his own path, Si." She stroked his chest while they talked. "You can't take the blame for him being there. It wasn't your fault."

"He'd already quit the rig that morning." Silas's confession crackled with guilt. "He didn't even work there anymore. He hung around to tell me he was leaving. He had a ticket out. A ticket home."

"Oh, Silas." Lucy nudged him toward the wicker loveseat. She propped him sideways on the cushion, his back resting against the arm so his leg extended the length of the bench. "That's awful. I'm so sorry."

"I'll live with it for the rest of my life." Her new lover drew her to him. She went willingly into his arms. She lay beside his brace—his other knee bent, his foot planted on the floor— and rested her head on his flat stomach.

"I only spoke to him once. That was enough to determine he cared for you very much, Si. He would have been glad *you* escaped. That *you* made it home."

"You're right, angel." He rested his palm in the dip of her waist, holding her close. "And that only makes it worse, doesn't it?"

"Not necessarily." She nibbled her lip as she chose her message carefully. "I think it means you owe him your best, though."

"I swear, Lucy, I'm going to make things right. I'm here for you, for Colby, for JD and Compass Ranch. I promise to do you proud. To keep you safe. To never disappoint you again. I'll do what's right, no matter how difficult it might be."

"And I'll be beside you every step. Colby too."

"I love you."

"Love you too."

She nuzzled his chest as they dozed together until the lights and purr of Colby's truck heading up the dirt road to their house extracted her from their hushed intimacy.

Lucy smiled as she imagined the three of them heading indoors to indulge their passion again or maybe staying right here and worshipping each other beneath the summer sky. She didn't expect the sudden tension morphing her pillow into a solid slab of flexed muscle.

"What the fuck happened to you?"

She inspected her husband when Silas's alarm infected her. Colby sported one hell of a shiner, a fat lip and a slice in his eyebrow that oozed blood. He spit over the railing, probably clearing the iron tang from his mouth.

"Nothing worth discussing." He grinned at Lucy then flexed his fingers into a loose fist. "I'm hoping you have some frozen peas stashed inside. I'm gonna need 'em."

She scooted off the loveseat and dashed into the kitchen. The rumbling of her men arguing, low and urgent, drifted through the open bathroom window as she gathered a couple other first aid supplies.

"It's not important. Some tool thought he could take out his ignorance on Billy. Made some asinine comment about the kid working for a homo. Billy fought back and the sheriff locked him up, but the dumb fuck wasn't ready to leave well enough alone. He must have been at The Soggy Boot. Saw me come for Billy then decided to go for another round."

"Son of a bitch!" Silas's curse cut through the night. "It's my fault this dickwad attacked you."

"You're so full of yourself." Colby attempted to take the sting out of the truth. "He was drunker than shit and looking for any excuse to start trouble."

"This jackass won't be the only one who has a problem with this..." Silas's voice trailed off.

"So I'll keep kicking asses and setting them straight. It's nobody's business who I fuck. Who I love."

"What will you do when someone attacks Lucy?" Silas's question faded then grew louder as though he paced with uneven hobbles. She hurried outside to calm him down. She could take care of herself, damn it.

"Silas Compton, stop this bullshit." She propped her hand on her hip. "You can't take responsibility for the whole universe."

"You two are my world. No one will hurt you because of me." He glared at her. "You should understand."

She threw the bag of peas at him, annoyed when he snatched it out of the air with ease and handed it to Colby. "It's not at all the same thing, Silas."

"It is." He adjusted his crutches then swung toward the stairs. "Colby, drive me into town. I'll confront these assholes myself. Then we'll talk. Maybe this isn't such a good idea after all."

"You swore you'd be here for us." She couldn't believe Silas would change his mind now. She'd never survive losing him.

"I swore to keep you safe."

Lucy watched until the taillights faded from sight before crumpling to the porch floor. Tears soaked her fingers as she covered her face and sobbed. He couldn't do this to them.

Not again.

Silas fumed the entire fifteen-minute trip into Compton Pass. Fury eradicated the opportunity to enjoy his first glimpse of the town he'd grown up in. Wrath blinded him to how it had evolved from a rural outpost into a bustling community, complete with an Internet café and an expanded school.

He refused to acknowledge Colby's attempts to woo him off the ledge. Fucked up leg or not, he planned to make a statement. A handful of titanium rods, screws and plates wouldn't stop him from protecting his family.

His lovers were not to be touched. Or there'd be hell to pay.

"Really, Si. This is ridiculous." Colby droned on above the country music spilling from the rowdy bar conveniently located behind the town's combo government building and two-celled jail as they swung into the gravel lot. "I don't need your sorry ass to fight my battles. Jones probably went home anyway."

"I'll check it out for myself." He slid from the bench seat of the pickup onto his good leg, ignoring how the jostling sent a tingle of pain up his spine.

"You're overdoing it today, Silas." Damn the observant foreman. "Let's go home. Lucy gives great massages."

"In a few." It had to be close to last call. Didn't a bunch of these cowboys have to be on the ranch in three or four hours? Hell, more than a couple probably started out the morning still tipsy or miserably hung-over.

He winced at the hypocritical disdain about to

cause him to pass judgment on guys he'd never even met. Fuck. He'd lived through ten years of rough mornings and still managed to perform at the head of the pack. Wyoming could easily be someone else's Alaska.

Colby stepped in front of him as he limped toward the front door.

"Are you sure you're okay to go in there?" True concern radiated from his lover for the first time since he'd shown up at the house with his face somewhat worse for wear. "With all the alcohol? Shit, I can smell it from here. You said..."

Now that Colby mentioned it, so could Silas. The fumes curdled his stomach.

"I remember what I asked of you." He sighed. "I'm alright. On that front anyway. Let me through, Colby."

"Fine."

Silas swung through the cracked door Colby held open as the other man mumbled beneath his breath.

"Stubborn. Egotistical. Overprotective..."

Silas headed straight toward the bar. Having left at eighteen, he'd never been inside The Soggy Boot but that didn't stop him. He'd familiarized himself with other less-than-fine establishments not so different than this since then. His eyes scanned the sparse crowd for the asshole who'd dared to threaten Colby, searching for a smirk or a confident leer he could wipe into the dirt.

Silas's stare made two circuits around the room before he quit. Only a smattering of half-passed-out men littered the place. None of them made good candidates for a bully. Shit, seemed as if the troublemaker had wised up and headed home after all. Damn.

"Didn't expect the pleasure of your company

again tonight, foreman." The bartender dried glasses to be put up for the night. "Thought you'd be home milking those scratches so that sweet little wife of yours would fix you up right."

"Not my idea." Colby leaned a hip against the bar, looking more tempting than he had a right to. "You remember Silas?"

"How could I forget that ugly mug? How the hell have you been?"

Silas abandoned his single-minded perusal, disappointed his prey had escaped. It took a couple beats for him to shave years off the man in front of him in his mind. If he removed the masculine set of his jaw, some of the laugh lines around his mouth and a foot or two of his height…

"Donnie?"

Colby and the other man cracked up.

"Nobody's called me that since high school." He grimaced. "Except my ma."

They'd had some fun times with the adventurous kid. How many others had he almost forgotten?

"I assume you hauled Stan Jenkins in, foreman?"

"Stan?" Colby shook his head, a confused glint in his eyes. Silas couldn't stand to wonder another second.

"I need to talk to the dude who messed with Colby."

"Dude?" Don laughed again. "Tonight keeps getting better and better."

"What the fuck's that supposed to mean?"

"Didn't he tell you? Four hands decided to gang up on our boy here. No idea what they were thinking. Colby's never had a problem holding his own. He kicked their asses good and hard. Then fired them on top of it all. Morons." Don chuckled as he recalled the situation, not in the least concerned. "Had to cut one off after you left as he tried to drown his sorrows. The other three couldn't make their hands or mouths work well enough to even try. Almost felt sorry for the bastards. Almost."

Colby winced. "I got carried away."

"No one expected different. Everybody knows you don't talk shit about Lucy around you. Or this fucker for that matter." Don jerked his chin in Silas's direction. "They had it coming."

A sickness swamped Silas's gut. Had he underestimated his lover?

Colby stared at him, waiting for his reaction. Oh shit, he'd nearly fucked this up again. They had to cut him some slack, right? He didn't have a decade of experience in how to be part of a relationship.

"You're right. They did." Silas turned to leave, calling over his shoulder, "Good to see you again, Don. I think Vicky and JD are planning a barbeque for the weekend. Come on over if you're free."

He'd reached the door when Colby paused to ask, "What was that you were saying about Stan Jenkins?"

Don stepped from behind the bar to avoid shouting. He lowered his voice until it wouldn't carry over the music blasting from the crappy speakers. "He said he was in the shitter when those four earned the smack down but he's a giant coward. I bet he hid in there on purpose. Afterward, he kept spouting off. The more he drank, the more he fired himself up. The fact no one else agreed pissed him off double."

The bartender scrubbed his hand through his hair then sighed hard. "I kicked him out after I heard him talking trash. About Lucy."

Don grimaced.

"We're rational men." Colby laid a hand on Don's shoulder then glared at Silas before adding, "Mostly. I won't let him punish the messenger. Spit it out."

"I told him he was no longer welcome here after I heard him say, 'If Colby ain't man enough for his wife, I'll give her a ride she won't soon forget. I'd have her screaming in no time.'"

"Motherfucker!" Silas smacked his crutch into the doorframe.

"I heard rumors he was the one who beat Beverly Morton last year, though the cops never did prove it. My waitresses refuse to serve him. He cornered Rae out in the parking lot one time. I don't care to think about what might have happened if I hadn't taken out the garbage right then. I don't like the bastard. I don't trust him. And I sure as shit didn't think you'd have appreciated the menace in his beady eyes as he insulted Lu. I thought maybe he'd tried something stupid."

"Fuck!" Colby slammed past him, out the door.

"Thanks, Don."

"I hope I'm wrong." The man wrung his dishtowel between his hands.

Silas cursed his jacked leg as he hobbled toward Colby. The man had already started the truck. Stray peas of gravel hit the side of the bar as he swung around in front of Si then slammed on the brakes. He leaned across the cab to push open the door. Silas tossed his crutches behind the seat, grabbed the oh-shit handle and clambered in. Not pretty but fast.

"Here. Call her." Colby tossed a cell phone into his lap.

Silas had the hunk of plastic halfway to his ear when it rang. He exchanged a look with Colby as the man took off at terrifying speeds given the road conditions and the obsidian darkness engulfing them as they left the radiance of the town behind.

Si wished he'd drive faster.

"What the hell are you boys doing out there?" JD's gruff reproach echoed loud enough for both of them to hear in the cab of the truck. "Do you know what time it is? Are you going to start acting like a bunch of dumbass teenagers 'cause you're all together again?"

"What do you mean?" Silas couldn't breathe past the constriction of his chest. "Because we went to The Boot? On a week night? Long story but Colby had to show some losers who's boss."

"Huh?" JD sounded like he might be running now. A car door slammed in the background. "You're not home? Neither of you?"

"No. We're heading back now though."

"Is Lucy with you?" his father shouted.

"No."

"God damn it!" JD cursed a blue streak. "My tires are flat, and I heard shots. Someone's unloading at your house. Woke me up the first time a few minutes ago. Heard two more rounds right before I dialed."

"We'll be there in five." At this rate they'd make it in half the time it'd taken to reach Compton Pass. Couldn't be soon enough. "We heard Stan Jenkins could be causing trouble."

"I should have fired that slimy jackass a long time ago. Never could catch him at anything I suspected," JD growled. "I'm gonna ride over. I'll come at the house from the back. Be careful. Both of you."

# Chapter Eleven

"If he harms one hair on her head, I'll kill that bastard painful and slow."

"Drive, Colby." Silas scrubbed his face with his hands, a calm settling low in the pit of his stomach. "She's tough and she's smart. We're no use if we don't make it there in one piece. We have to trust her to take care of herself until then."

Colby took his eyes from the road for an alarming second to stare at him as though he'd grown seven heads. "Who the fuck are you? What did you do with Silas?"

"I may be slow but I'm learning." He grinned as he selected *Home* from Colby's cell phone directory.

Ring.

Ring.

Ring.

"Answer!" Okay, so he hadn't quite obtained mastery of Zen-like patience. Redial. Wait. Redial. When voicemail kicked on for the third time, he disconnected with a snarl.

Colby zoomed through the gate marking the edge of Compass Ranch. Another minute and they'd be home. "I don't think it's a good idea to bring you into this mess. You'll be a sitting duck, Si."

"Don't waste time trying to make me leave this truck before we're in the yard. I may be fucked up but I can still kick your ass."

"We'll see about that some other time." Thankfully, Colby didn't continue to argue.

He cut the lights when they neared and, after they crested the hill, he killed the motor and put it in neutral. They rolled toward the house, their eyes adjusting to the blackness.

"Fuck! On the stairs." Silas pointed toward the figure creeping into the house. "Please tell me she has something to defend herself with."

Colby abandoned secrecy. He honked the horn and flashed his lights, doing anything possible to grant Lucy a heads up as they surged over the gap between them.

"We keep a shotgun loaded with rock-salt shells in a cabinet in the closet. I assume that's what JD heard before. But if she fired warning shots, I'm not sure how many cartridges she has left."

Silas opened the glove compartment and withdrew a revolver from the same spot his father had always stashed one. He checked to make sure it was ready to go then handed it to Colby as they screeched to a stop. "I'll be in behind you. As fast as I can."

Colby nodded then leapt from the truck, tearing up the stairs to the now open door. Before he'd finished taking the treads three at a time, a blast echoed from inside. Colby tripped. The sound shattering the night must have terrified him. He put one hand on the porch then kept running.

Silas cursed the entire journey into the house. He could hear shouting. All of it masculine. Where was Lucy? He slapped the light switch inside the kitchen, illuminating the chaos.

A man sprawled facedown on the kitchen floor.

Colby kept him pinned there with a knee between his shoulder blades. The back of the trespasser's shirt and pants were tattered and spotted with blood. The wounds didn't keep him from hollering as though he were nearly torn in two, though. "Keep her away from me. She shot me in the ass."

"You're lucky I didn't shoot your nasty dick off after all the bragging you did. Maybe you can tell all the guys in jail what a great lover you make. How you like to hurt your partner while you fuck. I'm sure you'll find someone willing to give you a taste of your own medicine." Lucy propped the shotgun against the kitchen table then flung herself into Silas's arms hard enough to knock him off balance.

"Shh." He cupped her head in his palm then tucked her against his chest. "You did fine. Better than. Brave. Smart. I'm proud of you, Lucy."

JD called out as he crossed through the living room, "It's me. Didn't see anyone out back. All clear."

"All clear," Silas repeated.

Colby cleaned the trash from their kitchen, accidentally kicking the asshole in the ribs as he escorted him outside to wait for the sheriff.

An hour later, Colby and Lucy signed affidavits swearing to the night's events on the hood of Compton Pass's single patrol car, which held Stan Jenkins in the backseat—sore but fine otherwise. Silas couldn't believe how old Sheriff Roberts, a friend of JD's, had gotten. Surely, the man should have retired by now. Guilt for denying both of them their rest warred with his impatience to have the matter resolved.

From the porch, his arms crossed over his chest, he thought of all he could do for Compass Ranch, his lovers and his family. Tonight had cemented his future.

Colby and Lucy held hands as they climbed to his

perch. JD and the sheriff ducked into the patrol car with a pair of nods. He lifted one hand in a subtle wave as they carted Stan to jail.

On the horizon, the barest hint of sunrise lightened the sky.

"I should be tired, but I'm wide awake." Lucy sighed as she sank to the wicker loveseat beside him.

"Good. I need to talk to you two." Silas hated the dread creasing Colby's brow and the coldness freezing Lucy's pretty blue eyes into a decent imitation of an Alaskan glacier.

"I swear to God if you make one stupid comment, I'll go berserk." Lucy glared at him.

"What if I tell you both that I've been a complete moron?" He enjoyed the shock turning her pouty lips into a perfect circle.

"I'd have to agree." Colby winced as he tested the puffiness around his eye. "But for some stupid reason, we love you anyway."

"I'm sorry." He offered the only apology he could summon. How could he describe how much he regretted all the time he'd wasted by refusing to believe they were strong enough to handle their situation, the ups and downs, and protect themselves in the meantime? "So sorry. The perfection of the two of you together blinded me. I didn't dream big enough, that the circle could include all three of us and not break. I was terrified I'd destroy you both. All of us, really. I can't believe how insulting that was. Christ, I *am* a fucking moron."

He wished Colby could join them. The loveseat wasn't large enough. He bolted upright, balancing on his good leg, then scooped Lucy into his arms. Colby understood what he intended as though the man could read his heart and mind. He probably could.

After tonight, Silas swore he'd never doubt them

again.

Before he could ask, Colby tugged the cushion from the furniture onto the decking. The other man took Lucy from him long enough to give Silas a hand down. Then he settled her beside Silas before joining them on the ground, one lover bracketing each side of his body.

They leaned in toward him.

"You're noble and proud, even if misguided sometimes." Lucy placed a tender kiss on his lips. He wrapped his arm around her thin waist and indulged in a taste of heaven.

"Too strong for your own good. To distance yourself so long and shoulder everyone else's burdens. You have to invite us in. Allow us to help. Let us be there for you." Colby nudged his wife aside to stake his claim. "Shit, yeah. I love that."

Silas agreed. Rough skin abraded his face and the brute force of the man's tongue as it plundered his mouth fired him up.

Lucy returned, licking the intersection of their mouths until they joined in a three-way kiss that tasted like perfection. While they explored each other, someone slipped a hand beneath the waistband of Silas's shorts to encircle his cock. Before long another hand joined in.

Colby cupped Silas's balls in his calloused palm while Lucy stroked his shaft with her dainty fingers. He surrendered, granting them free rein. Whatever they wished for—whatever they craved—they could have from him. Now and forever.

The early morning air caressed his thighs when someone whisked his shorts off. Pressure built on his good thigh. Colby relinquished his hold on Silas's mouth to nestle between his legs instead.

"Oh, fuck." Silas gasped into Lucy's smile when Colby licked around his wife's fingers, stealing his first taste of erect cock.

"I was thinking more along the lines of suck. But I have no idea how to do this."

"What do you like?" Lucy coached her husband as though Silas weren't there. "Start with that."

She angled Silas's cock toward Colby's parted lips, encouraging him to experiment. The man reached his tongue out and licked the drop of pearly fluid from the tip. A simple act. One guaranteed to jumpstart Silas's libido.

"Get naked, Lu," he ordered, not entirely able to suppress his dominant tendencies. "Give me a taste of you while you teach him."

She stripped the jeans she'd thrown on in a flash when the sheriff arrived then knelt with one knee on either side of his head so she faced her husband, who had graduated to sucking on the tip of Silas's cock.

Si wrapped his hands around her hips then tugged her pussy to his face. He inhaled deeply, relishing the scent of his mate's arousal before he allowed himself to feast on the delicacy. She writhed in his hold, smearing her juices on his cheeks as he chased her clit until he latched onto the sensitive nub. He swirled his tongue around it, soothing her initial cries into moans.

When she'd calmed, she mentored her husband. She leaned forward, adjusting the angle of Colby's lips on Silas's cock so Silas glided to the back of the man's hot mouth. Fuck! Silas's hips jerked, forcing the head of his hard-on to slip into Colby's throat. When the man gagged, he backed off. Lucy soothed her husband while stroking Silas's cock.

After a few seconds, Colby reclaimed his position, swallowing Silas's full length with ease this time. He relaxed, massaging Silas's erection with involuntary muscles.

Silas renewed his attention to Lucy's pussy,

lapping at the sweetness flowing more freely from her delicate channel. Every time Colby hit a particularly pleasurable spot on his cock, he rewarded Lucy's coaching. Soon, the man had honed in on what Silas preferred and drove him rapidly toward eruption.

Silas trembled beneath their combined assault then redoubled his oral play. Lucy laughed, then groaned. Colby abandoned Silas's cock for an instant to cheer him on. "Yeah, more. Make her come, Silas. She's gorgeous like this. Right on the edge."

He slid his hands from her hips to her breasts. At the same time he rolled her hard nipples in his fingers, he jabbed his tongue as deep as it would go in her tiny pussy. She bucked on his face, making him work to maintain contact throughout her explosive orgasm.

When she settled, he cleaned her with small licks of his relaxed tongue until she climbed to her feet.

"Going somewhere?" Colby asked when Silas could only stare at the sight revealed to him. His powerful, respected best friend lounged between his legs, eagerly devouring Silas's cock.

Even his dreams hadn't seemed so erotic.

"Be right back, don't you worry." Lucy smacked her husband's ass—when had Colby shucked his clothes?—then sashayed inside, calling over her shoulder, "Make him good and ready, I want to ride him."

"Don't think that's a problem." Colby swallowed Silas's cock once more then chuckled, the vibrations nearly launching him into the stratosphere.

Lucy might have been gone hours, though it probably only seemed like it, leaving Silas stretched on a rack of pleasure. When she returned, she tapped Colby on the shoulder. "Turnabout is fair play, right, Silas?"

Before his mind could fully process her intent,

Colby scaled Silas's supine body and presented his cock. Without thinking, Silas's mouth opened, inviting the man inside. The instant his lips encircled the shaft, a spurt of precome decorated his tongue. He swallowed, thrilling them both.

"That's right, Si." Lucy praised him. She straddled Silas's hips as she fit his cock to the mouth of her dripping pussy. "Take him deep like he did for you. From here, I have a nice view of his ass."

Silas groaned. His entire universe consisted of Colby, Lucy and the rapture they gifted him. Colby filled his mouth, giving him something to suck on, taste, explore with his tongue. Lucy used her wicked pussy to keep his cock happy. More than. God, he couldn't hold out long like this. Not with everything he'd ever hoped for in his reach.

"Suck him good, Silas, and I'll prepare him for you." She tempted Silas with dirty promises as she bounced on his cock. The stranglehold her inner muscles had on his erection couldn't fool him. She loved every instant as much as he did. "You'd like to fuck us both, back to back, wouldn't you?"

"Mmph." Colby's veined shaft muffled Silas's agreement. The blunt crown grew more defined against his tongue. His lover would surrender soon. He'd make sure of it.

Silas imagined all the tricks Red had used on him during the long, cold nights. He wriggled his tongue, massaging the underside of Colby's cock. The pitch of his lover's groans escalated. The snick of the cap on the lube bottle, which Lucy must have retrieved from the bedside table, cut through the night.

Colby inserted his cock to the base between Silas's lips. The man's wife must be making good on her promises. Silas wished he could see her tiny fingers probing her husband's back passage, loosening him for

Silas's invasion.

Their plan worked a little too well.

"I think he's \ ready, Silas." Lucy shivered. "I have almost my whole hand in him now."

Silas caught the tensing of Colby's sac on his chin but there was nothing he could do to halt the inevitable. Instead he tipped his head back, opening his throat to accept the giant load Colby pumped into him, spurt after spurt. He gulped, surprised to find he enjoyed the salty tang of the other man's ecstasy.

He gouged Colby's legs when Lucy followed suit, coming hard on his embedded cock. She rode him fast, grinding her slight weight on him with rock after rock. When Colby would have withdrawn, she perked up once more.

"No." A sharp slap rang through the early morning. "Don't move."

Silas froze as well.

Lucy laughed. "Not you. Keep sucking, Silas. Colby will get hard again, if you do it right. Just like me. If I keep fucking you, I'll be horny again in no time."

Silas gripped Colby's ass to pin his lover close then made it his personal mission to rejuvenate the man. He had an idea. A naughty, decadent, delicious idea.

Either he was a better cocksucker than he thought or Colby had saved up a bunch of unfulfilled dreams of his own. In no more than a few minutes, the man sported a full hard-on once more. Impressive.

"Lu, I need him in my ass. I'll take care of you after, I swear, but I need…"

She swung her leg over Silas's hips, sliding off his length as she went.

"Ah!"

"Don't worry. Colby's going to finish you off, Si. You seemed to enjoy his ass before." The sparkle in her eye proved she'd enjoyed watching them fuck just as much.

Colby withdrew his cock from Silas's mouth then inched down his torso. Colby kept backing up until the stiff length of Silas's dick nestled between the cheeks of his ass.

Lucy fisted Silas's cock. "So thick. So huge."

She held him still for Colby, who descended, engulfing him in heat so much quicker than the gradual penetration he'd orchestrated earlier. Within moments, Colby squatted over him and began to fuck. Powerful thighs flexed to lift and lower the man. The motion caused his cock to bob and dance.

Lucy played with her pussy with one hand then took her husband's shaft in the other. Colby slammed his eyes closed when she began a skilled massage over the crown, slippery with Silas's spit and Colby's precome.

"You want it. Don't you, sweetheart?" Silas forced himself to segregate the section of his brain engulfed in fireworks to ensure Lucy's pleasure. As much as he'd love for the heat of Colby's come to spray over his chest, their woman had to have more.

"So bad." Lucy moaned. "When you're finished. I want him to fuck me. Hard. Fast."

"No." Silas grinned when they both threw him a curious look. "Not later. Now."

He put his hands beneath her arms then tugged her over him. Colby clearly understood when her cute ass lined up with his cock. They partnered to position her with her back to Colby's front, straddling Silas.

The next time Colby lunged upward, his cock pierced his wife's wet opening.

"Oh, my God." She shuddered in their grip. "Do it again, Colby. Please. Please, fuck me."

Silas held her shoulders forward while Colby

urged her to drop her hips

"Oh shit, yes. He's fucking me. Deeper. Everytie."

Silas pictured the head of Colby's cock tucked into her folds more thoroughly on every upstroke. Silas couldn't resist the temptation of Lucy's swaying breasts. He lunged up to capture her nipple in his mouth. He bit gently on the tip, causing her back to arch and Colby to burrow farther into her swollen tissue.

"Again!" she screamed.

Colby obliged, fucking them both in counterpoint.

Such divine rapture had to be fleeting.

A few more strokes and Colby's quivering thighs betrayed him.

Silas paused his attention to Lucy's tits to give her warning. "Your husband is about to come. Deep inside you, while holding me tight. Are you ready? Can you come with him? I'd die to hear you both. Loud. Strong. Do it. Give me your satisfaction."

Before he'd finished his request, Colby roared. He lost control, his evaporated timidity proving he forgot to be careful of Silas's thigh, as if Silas cared. Colby slammed his ass onto Silas's cock, grinding so the head nudged Colby's gland. At the same time, Colby contracted his arms, squeezing Lucy close, impaling her as fully as he could. She stopped breathing then screamed as she shattered, coming around her husband, on top of their lover.

Colby's ass hugged Silas's cock over and over as he emptied himself in his wife. The beauty of their unified completion forced Silas to join them. No way could he resist pure perfection.

He put one hand on Colby's thigh and the other over Lucy's heart as he poured himself into Colby's heated depths. He'd never come as hard or as long as he did beneath the orgasm assaulting him then. The bond between the three of them felt as tangible as the cushion beneath him.

For a moment he thought their devotion might be visible too.

And then he realized the sun rose behind his lovers, bathing them all in the light of a new day.

# Epilogue

Silas shook his head when JD offered him a beer, snagging a Coke from the bucket of ice instead. "I'm good with this, thanks."

He twisted the top off the bottle then sighed as he surveyed the crowd gathering to celebrate his homecoming. A bunch of the attendees joined them to support Colby and Lucy instead. They hardly knew Silas but the subtle congratulations proved all the friends his lovers had accumulated in the past decade could tell the pair had finally gotten what they really wanted.

The triad didn't make a big production out of the fact that they intended to share more than burgers and potato salad at their simple barbeque. But Lucy in her gorgeous white summer dress, Colby sporting a perma-grin, and the pile of presents overflowing the table near the appetizers made it clear those who loved them all understood the significance of the day.

Understood and supported.

Silas couldn't believe how different his life seemed now than a few short months ago. So many amazing changes almost obscured the pain—of his healing body, of losing Red, of dealing with his father, who still refused to visit a doctor.

If only his brothers were here, things would be as close to perfect as possible.

Vicky beamed at him as she approached. "It's like old times, Silas."

"I'm sorry." He'd ached to apologize for years. Lucy looked over at him and smiled, lending him her strength to continue. "If I hadn't gone, maybe none of the others would have followed. I see now how wrong I was. How much I wasted. I'm sorry."

"Shush." His mother hugged him, drying her eyes on his shirt. "Each of you had to choose your own way. I'm just thankful you found a path home."

"I'm thankful home was still waiting for me."

Colby had a group of kids laughing as he flipped burgers high into the air. Lucy zipped around, greeting guests and brightening the summer with her smile. Cindi chatted with Leah Hollister in the corner, and Don was welcomed with a round of slaps on the back from Jake along with a bunch of the other ranch hands.

The buzz of the party died down when a new arrival climbed from a rental car. Silas dropped his arm from his mother's shoulder, preparing for the thrilled shriek to follow.

Vicky didn't disappoint.

Her surprise didn't keep her frozen. Instead, she high-tailed it for the yard where she launched herself at her second oldest son. Seth caught their mother in mid-air, returning her hug with interest.

While everyone's attention focused on the reunion, JD glared in Silas's direction.

"Sorry," Silas mouthed.

His father closed his eyes for a moment then shook it off, as though agreeing to a truce. They'd enjoy the party. With half his sons on Compass Ranch, it was a rare day. A day to celebrate.

Tomorrow, they'd tackle the rest. Together.

## What Happens Next?

If you've enjoyed the Compass Brothers so far, don't wait to find out what happens to them next in Southern Comfort.

Caught between desire and a promise…

Compass Brothers, Book 2

Seth Compton knew from the first that his boss's daughter was all wrong for him. She was too feisty, too damned independent and, at seven years his junior, too damned young. When she comes home with a college diploma and fiancé on her arm, though, he can't quite remember all the reasons he held her at arm's length.

It's not just his jeans-tightening reaction to her all-grown-up curves. Something doesn't feel right about her impending marriage, and he won't rest until he's stopped her from making the biggest mistake of her life.

The morning after her wild bachelorette party, Jody expected a hangover. The surprise? Waking up tied to a bed with sexy-as-sin Seth. He's got some wild idea about proving they belong together, but she's not buying it. Besides, she has a promise to keep that's too close to her heart to risk, especially not with a man who, until now, made his disinterest plain.

No one ever said Seth backed down from a challenge. She's going to make him work for it? No problem. Luckily for him, he has plenty of rope…

Warning: This story contains a bondage lovin' cowboy who kidnaps and hogties a cowgirl to his bed and does all sorts of naughty things to her. Fun, right?

## An Excerpt From Southern Comfort:

"Welcome home, Jody." He stepped forward and bent down to give her a hug. Her shoulder-length chestnut-brown hair smelled like honeysuckle. He had to force himself to keep the embrace quick and brotherly. His cock stirred, and he closed his eyes briefly, trying to ignore the usual arousal that accompanied her arrival. She was the boss's daughter and even at twenty-one, she was too damn young for him.

She'd been a tomboyish twelve-year-old when he first came to work on the ranch and the other hands had given him shit when it became obvious the young girl had a crush on him. Her infatuation hadn't abated until last Christmas, when he'd foolishly kissed her under the mistletoe and then shoved her away.

Since then, the easy camaraderie and innocent flirting they'd engaged in since her graduation from high school had evaporated. She'd only been home once since Christmas, but he could see in her face she was still angry with him. He was determined now that she was back to stay, he'd make things right again. He'd been thinking about her return a lot lately. Things were about to change between him and the little wildcat. He grinned at the thought.

"Thanks, Seth. Good to be back."

"Didn't get the impression you were staying," Thomas muttered.

"Daddy. Don't you think you were kind of rude to Paul?"

"Paul?" Seth asked.

"I mean we only just got here and told you our good news."

Thomas frowned. "Is that what we're calling it?"

Jody's eyes narrowed. "Yes, it is. Didn't you tell

me you wanted me to find a nice man and settle down?"

"What the—" Seth crossed his arms over his chest, suddenly worried about the direction of this conversation. "You were pissed as shit when Thomas gave you that advice. Said women these days didn't need a man to be happy and you didn't plan to ever get hitched." The fight she and her father had had at the end of last summer was epic. Seth had tried to stay out of it, mind his own business, but when Jody and Thomas went toe to toe, it was hard not to hear. Neither of them understood the concept of *inside* voices.

Jody glanced at him and gave him a small smile that seemed too sad to be genuine. "Turns out I was wrong."

Seth fought to restrain a growl from escaping his chest. She'd brought home a man? Paul? Seth's fists clenched at the thought. "How so?"

Thomas shrugged, the helpless gesture at odds with his legendary ability to handle anything. Of course, now that Seth thought about it, Jody was the exception to her father's confident approach to life. Her mother had died when she was five, and Thomas had struggled to understand and raise his daughter since then.

Jody lifted her left hand, flashing a diamond the size of Dallas in his face. "I'm engaged."

"The hell you are." The words left Seth's mouth before he could catch them. While Thomas laughed at his reply, he could see he'd sent Jody's temper into orbit.

She retracted her hand and studied the ring, sarcasm dripping from her tone. "Really? I'm not engaged? Because I think this ring and the fact Paul got down on one knee and said, 'Will you marry me?' sort of proves that I am."

"Who the fuck is this Paul character?" Seth took

two steps toward the main house, ready to confront the asshole who'd dared to propose without even bothering to meet her family first, but Jody stepped in front of him, stopping him.

"Back off, Seth. You know perfectly well who Paul is. He's been my best friend since freshmen year of college."

"*That* Paul? What the fuck? I thought he was gay. Hell, he spent his entire last visit here flirting with the ranch hands."

Jody closed her eyes and took a deep breath. But long before a ten count, she replied, through gritted teeth, "Obviously, he's not gay."

"Since when?"

"Since he fucking proposed to me. Why am I even having this conversation? This is none of your damn business."

He bent down until his face was mere inches from hers. "Is that right? Well, I beg to differ."

She leaned closer, and he could detect the slight scent of chocolate on her breath. Jody clearly hadn't lost her sweet tooth, though he was beginning to wonder where she'd misplaced her common sense. "You are not my boyfriend and you are not my brother. Hell, you're not a part of this freaking family at all. You are my father's foreman, which means my decision to get married is none of your damn business."

He struggled to keep his hands on his hips, rather than reach over and prove to Miss Jody Kirkland how very wrong she was. His fingers were itching to take her over his knee and spank some sense into her.

She'd made herself his business the very first day he'd come to work here and she'd climbed atop Coy, her father's newest addition to the stable. The far-from-tamed horse had taken exception to its rider and bolted across the yard, jumping a fence and sprinting across the lower pasture. Seth had chased her on Charlton for close to a mile before managing to catch up and pull the fool girl off the runaway roan.

He could still recall the way she'd trembled in his arms and looked at him like he'd hung the moon for rescuing her. By the time they'd returned to the stable, they were laughing like old friends and his position at the ranch had been solidified. As he looked into her blue eyes now, he missed the admiration and wished to hell he could get rid of the anger that had crept in instead.

"Jody," Thomas broke in. "You know full well I consider Seth a part of this family. If he takes exception to your asinine engagement, then perhaps you should listen to why."

Jody released a furious breath. "You can't object to a man who's been my friend for years."

Seth leaned back a bit. "Don't you think it's a little strange that one minute the guy's gay and the next he's not?"

"He never said he was gay."

"That's not something we needed to be told. It was kind of obvious. Is he bi?" Seth could understand bisexuality. He'd seen glimpses of it in his older brother, Silas, when they were growing up and he suspected now that his brother was back home in Wyoming, Silas would be acting on some of the feelings he had for his best friend, Colby.

Jody sighed loudly. "No. He's in love with me. Just me."

Seth knocked his hat against his jeans in frustration. "Never heard you talk about him like he was your boyfriend. You were home for Easter, Jody, and you didn't say one word about dating him. When did this so-called love affair start?"

"It turned into something more than friendship

recently."

He tried to beat down the twinge of jealousy that accompanied the thought of her being *more than friends* with any other man. She was right. He had no claim staked on her. But it sure as hell felt like he did. "So why the rush? If you've only started dating, I don't see why—"

"Because I want to. I don't need any more reason than that."

"Just like that?" Seth tried to understand what the hell was going on inside her pretty head. The only thing missing from her haughty proclamation was for her to stamp her foot on the ground like a three-year-old. She wasn't like this. She'd never been a spoiled girl, never been prone to temper tantrums or selfish demands. She'd been a fun-loving tomboy who'd grown into his laughing, easygoing friend. This angry woman was a stranger to him, and he missed the real Jody.

"That's right. And we're not waiting. We came home to have the ceremony performed here."

"When exactly?"

Thomas cleared his throat. Bewilderment crossed his boss's face. He was sure the same confusion resided on his. There would be no help from that camp. "They plan to bring the justice of the peace out to make it official here at the ranch in two weeks."

Hell to the no! Seth would see her married to some stranger only over his dead body. He started to say exactly the same thing, but the argument that came out was much different than what he'd intended. "What about love, Jody? Do you love him?"

His softly spoken question seemed to jar her a bit and for just a second, he saw the trace of his old friend before she disappeared again behind the indifferent, cold woman who'd replaced her.

"What kind of question is that?"

Thomas leaned against the horse stall and crossed his arms over his chest. "A pretty valid one, if you ask me."

Jody turned to look at her father and shook her head. "You two really are a matched set, you know that? Way to gang up on me."

"Answer me, Jody," Seth persisted. "Are you in love?"

She studied his face and a glimmer of pain shone in her eyes. Then she nodded, turned on her heel and walked out of the stable.

It wasn't until she disappeared around the corner that it began to sink in. Seth had missed his chance with her. He'd pushed her away for too long.

"You realize you made a mistake there, right?" Thomas asked.

Seth nodded sadly. Mistake was putting it lightly. He'd fucked up. Big time. "Yeah. I guess I did."

Thomas studied his face and then chuckled. "Think we're talking about two different things. Of course, maybe not. She may be in love, son, but she didn't say with who."

# About the Authors

Jayne Rylon and Mari Carr met at a writing conference in June 2009 and instantly became arch enemies. Two authors couldn't be more opposite. Mari, when free of her librarian-by-day alter ego, enjoys a drink or two or... more. Jayne, allergic to alcohol, lost huge sections her financial-analyst mind to an epic explosion resulting from Mari gloating about her hatred of math. To top it off, they both had works in progress with similar titles and their heroes shared a name. One of them would have to go.

The battle between them for dominance was a bloody, but short one, when they realized they'd be better off combining their forces for good (or smut). With the ink dry on the peace treaty, they emerged as good friends, who have a remarkable amount in common despite their differences, and their writing partnership has flourished. Except for the time Mari attempted to poison Jayne with a bottle of Patron. Accident or retaliation? You decide.

Join Mari's newsletter and Jayne's Naughty News so you don't miss new releases, contests, or exclusive subscriber-only content._

## Also by Jayne Rylon

MEN IN BLUE
*Hot Cops Save Women In Danger*
Night is Darkest
Razor's Edge
Mistress's Master
Spread Your Wings
Wounded Hearts
Bound For You

DIVEMASTERS
*Sexy SCUBA Instructors By Day, Doms On A Mega-Yacht By Night*
Going Down
Going Deep
Going Hard

POWERTOOLS
*Five Guys Who Get It On With Each Other & One Girl. Enough Said?*
Kate's Crew
Morgan's Surprise
Kayla's Gift
Devon's Pair
Nailed to the Wall
Hammer it Home

HOT RODS
*Powertools Spin Off. Keep up with the Crew plus...*
*Seven Guys & One Girl. Enough Said?*
King Cobra
Mustang Sally
Super Nova
Rebel on the Run

Swinger Style
Barracuda's Heart
Touch of Amber
Long Time Coming

STANDALONE
*Menage*
4-Ever Theirs
Nice & Naughty
*Contemporary*
Where There's Smoke
Report For Booty

COMPASS BROTHERS
*Modern Western Family Drama Plus Lots Of Steamy Sex*
Northern Exposure
Southern Comfort
Eastern Ambitions
Western Ties

COMPASS GIRLS
*Daughters Of The Compass Brothers Drive Their Dads Crazy And Fall In Love*
Winter's Thaw
Hope Springs
Summer Fling
Falling Softly

PLAY DOCTOR
*Naughty Sexual Psychology Experiments Anyone?*
Dream Machine
Healing Touch

RED LIGHT
*A Hooker Who Loves Her Job*
Complete Red Light Series Boxset
FREE - Through My Window - FREE
Star
Can't Buy Love
Free For All

PICK YOUR PLEASURES
*Choose Your Own Adventure Romances!*
Pick Your Pleasure
Pick Your Pleasure 2

RACING FOR LOVE
*MMF Menages With Race-Car Driver Heroes*
Complete Series Boxset
Driven
Shifting Gears

PARANORMALS
*Vampires, Witches, And A Man Trapped In A Painting*
Paranormal Double Pack Boxset
Picture Perfect
Reborn

## Look for these titles by Mari Carr

**Big Easy**
Blank Canvas
Crash Point
Full Position
Rough Draft
Triple Beat
Winner Takes All
Going Too Fast

**Boys of Fall:**
Free Agent
Red Zone
Wild Card

**Compass:**
Northern Exposure
Southern Comfort
Eastern Ambitions
Western Ties
Winter's Thaw
Hope Springs
Summer Fling
Falling Softly

**Farepoint Creek:**
Outback Princess
Outback Cowboy
Outback Master
Outback Lovers

**June Girls:**
No Recourse
No Regrets

**Just Because:**
Because of You
Because You Love Me
Because It's True

**Lowell High:**
Bound by the Past
Covert Affairs
Mad about Meg

**Bundles**
Cowboy Heat
Sugar and Spice
Madison Girls
Scoundrels

**Second Chances:**
Fix You
Dare You
Just You
Near You
Reach You
Always You

**Sparks in Texas:**
Sparks Fly
Waiting for You
Something Sparked
Off Limits
No Other Way
Whiskey Eyes

**Trinity Masters:**
Elemental Pleasure
Primal Passion
Scorching Desire
Forbidden Legacy
Hidden Devotion
Elegant Seduction
Secret Scandal
Delicate Ties

**Wild Irish:**
Come Monday
Ruby Tuesday
Waiting for Wednesday
Sweet Thursday
Friday I'm in Love
Saturday Night Special
Any Given Sunday
Wild Irish Christmas
January Girl
February Stars

**Individual Titles:**
Seducing the Boss
Tequila Truth
Erotic Research
Rough Cut
Happy Hour
Power Play
One Daring Night
Assume the Positions
Slam Dunk

## What Was Your Favorite Part?

Did you enjoy this book? If so, please leave a review and tell your friends about it. Word of mouth and online reviews are immensely helpful and greatly appreciated.

## Jayne's Shop

Check out Jayne's online shop for autographed print books, direct download ebooks, reading-themed apparel up to size 5XL, mugs, tote bags, notebooks, Mr. Rylon's wood (you'll have to see it for yourself!) and more.

www.jaynerylon.com/shop

# Listen Up!

The majority of Jayne's books are also available in audio format on Audible, Amazon and iTunes.

Made in the USA
Lexington, KY
02 October 2018